VIRUS

Molly Brown

SCHOLASTIC

Scholastic Children's Books,
Scholastic Publications Ltd,
7–9 Pratt Street, London NW1 0AE, UK

Scholastic Inc.,
555 Broadway, New York, NY 10012–3999, USA

Scholastic Canada Ltd,
123 Newkirk Road, Richmond Hill,
Ontario, Canada L4C 3G5

Ashton Scholastic Pty Ltd,
PO Box 579, Gosford, New South Wales,
Australia

Ashton Scholastic Ltd,
Private Bag 92801, Penrose, Auckland,
New Zealand

First published in the UK by Scholastic Publications Ltd, 1994

Text copyright © Molly Brown, 1994

ISBN 0 590 55816 1

Typeset by DP Photosetting, Aylesbury, Bucks
Printed by Cox & Wyman Ltd, Reading, Berks

10 9 8 7 6 5 4 3 2 1

To Jessica Palmer, who gave me a shove when I
needed it.

CONTENTS

PROLOGUE

Evanston, Illinois, 2009

In a suburban house not far from a university campus, a small, dark-haired woman paced up and down her living-room floor. It was early afternoon, but the curtains were drawn and the house was dark and full of shadows. The woman stopped her relentless pacing for a moment and froze, listening.

She walked over to the window, and pulled a tiny section of curtain away from the glass – just enough to see, but not be seen. A crowd of people – hundreds of them, young and old, rich and poor – advanced down her suburban street, waving banners and shouting her name. A squad of uniformed police stood in a line across her front lawn, riot shields at the ready.

She jumped at the sound of footsteps behind her,

and turned to face her husband. "Don't let it get to you, April," he said. "What we're doing is too important."

"I know."

"And we're so close..."

"We're not just close," she corrected him. "We've done it. We've actually done it."

"What? You mean...?"

She nodded, a gleam of triumph in her eyes. "It's alive."

PART 1

A Temporary Assignment

Chicago, Illinois, 2078

Amanda saw the building as soon as she came out of the subway. It was one of those old factories that had been converted into offices at least a hundred years before, when there'd been the need for that sort of thing. At least there were windows; so few buildings had windows these days.

She hoped she looked all right. She'd bought her retro black knee-length polyester skirt and white blouse specially, since her wardrobe was full of old-fashioned see-through metallic wraparound tunics that had been out of style for at least a dozen years. Hand-me-downs from her aunt, who had insisted that she hold on to them because they were bound to come back into style someday. "Everything always comes back," her aunt used to tell her. "That's the one thing you can always depend on: everything comes back."

She ran her fingers through her hair and straightened her skirt. Then she took a deep breath and walked inside.

A standard metal security robot sat behind a large counter in the lobby, surrounded by video screens which displayed a continually changing view of the building's exterior from every conceivable angle. A separate set of screens showed the unchanging scenery of the empty lobbies upstairs. On the counter in front of the robot, there was a single old-fashioned candlestick telephone. The robot nodded to her as she pushed her way through the revolving door.

"Help you, Miss?" it asked in an old man's voice.

For a moment, Amanda was almost too startled to answer. Of course, she'd seen robot receptionists before. Most places of business had them. But in all her eighteen years she'd never seen one like this. It was made out of steel, like all the others she had seen. It had the same large camera lens eyes and small motionless mouth. But instead of the usual grey jumpsuit, it was dressed in a faded red doorman's uniform, complete with frayed gold braid on the shoulders and across the front of its hat. Talk about retro-dressing!

"I said can I help you, Miss?"

"Oh, sorry. I'm expected at Hawk Engineering. The

Crane Agency sent me." She removed her dark glasses.

The robot's camera eyes stared at her without expression.

"I'm a temp," she added.

"Okey, dokey, Miss. Let me just get them on the line." The robot slowly reached its thin arm out to the candlestick telephone, and lifted it as if it were a great weight. It pressed the receiver down a couple of times until it got a dial tone, and then with a finger that she would almost describe as "boney", it dialled four digits. After a few moments, the robot said, "Hullo? Hawk Engineering? Got a young lady down here in the lobby, says she's a temp from the ..." it leaned forward ... "what'd you say was the name of your company, honey?"

"The Crane Agency."

"She says she's from Crane," the robot said into the phone.

Someone on the other end said something she couldn't hear, and then the robot seemed to laugh. It was a weary, rasping sound that came from somewhere deep within its metal chest, having no connection whatsoever with its motionless speaker of a mouth. "Heh heh heh. No, not bad," the robot added in a confidential tone of voice. "Bit of a cutie, I'd say ... petite, with long brown hair. I'll send her on up then."

She had to walk up to the third floor, because the

elevator, the robot told her, was "on the fritz". There were only two doors on the third floor, each on opposite ends of the long, narrow corridor. Neither had any sort of window. The only source of light in the hallway was one bare bulb hanging from the ceiling by a slightly frayed-looking wire.

Despite the dimness of the hall, she saw that one of the doors had a small sign with some writing on it. She walked towards that one. As she approached it, she could see that the lettering spelled the words: "Hawk Engineering: Radioactive Decontamination A Speciality". She knocked three times, loudly. No reply. She twisted the knob and managed, after a bit of a struggle, to open the door. She found herself staring into a large, dark room with no furniture except for three empty desks, covered in dust and cobwebs.

"Hello!" she called into the darkness. Again no reply. She shut the door and headed down to the other end of the corridor.

She glanced up at the video camera mounted on the wall next to the broken lift, and saw it swivel around to follow her.

The door at the other end had no writing on it at all. She knocked and waited. When there was no reply again, she opened the door and stepped inside. Again, she saw some empty desks. But this time, she heard a faint hum coming from somewhere. "Hello!" she called out. "Anybody here?"

"You the temp?"

"Where are you?"

"Over here." A small man with tousled curly blonde hair and large wire-rimmed spectacles popped his head around a doorway. "We're all in here."

She walked towards him carefully. "This is Hawk Engineering, isn't it?"

"It better be," he told her, "or I'm in the wrong office."

She walked towards the man and saw that he was sitting in front of a computer terminal in a huge room that was full of them. There were rows and rows of desks, each with its own computer terminal, but hardly any people. She doubted there were half a dozen people in the whole place.

"I'm supposed to ask for Christine," she began.

"Christine's off sick," the man interrupted. "But I'll take care of you. What's your name?"

"Amanda. Amanda Carter."

"I'm Steve Wilson. Just call me Steve. You worked much with computers?"

"You want the truth?"

"Ooh," Steve said with a mock grimace. "But you must have used one?"

"I have a small one at home. Just big enough to send and receive electronic mail and radio transmissions, handle the bills, and time the oven. You know the sort of thing ... cheap and cheerful. The agency said this was just going to be VDU work, like typing. I *can* type," she added nervously, "a bit. I mean, I type at home. On my computer; it used to belong to my aunt." Shut up, Amanda, she scolded herself. You're talking too much.

Steve nodded, a knowing look on his face. "This is your first job, isn't it?"

Amanda looked down at her feet, embarrassed. "Is it really that obvious?"

"I'm sure you'll have no problems," Steve said reassuringly. "Working here was my first job, too."

She looked up and saw that he was smiling at her. Steve had a big, broad grin that made his whole face light up. He looked young – genuinely young. Almost as young as her. The skin on his face didn't have that tight look most people acquired after decades of anti-ageing treatments. But no, Amanda told herself, he isn't young at all – he can't be – he's just had a better series of treatments than most people could afford. In all her life, she'd never met anyone even remotely near her own age.

She'd spent most of her life on her uncle's farm, and no one lived within a hundred and fifty miles of him. But even when he got a job overseas and she went to live with his sister who'd moved to Chicago – her Aunt Marti – she still didn't meet many people. The One Day War fifty years earlier had left few survivors. Amanda's father and his family had only survived that catastrophic day because they'd lived on an isolated farm in the middle of nowhere.

And the population was still falling. Most people were sterile after the war, and the few that weren't often gave birth to mutants who didn't live very long. Amanda's parents had been exceptions. Neither of them were sterile, and Amanda had been born normal and healthy. But her mother died when Amanda was still a baby, and her father died a couple of years after that, leaving her to be raised by her father's brother and sister.

Her aunt used to tell her there were *some* young people – even little children – in the city. But so far Amanda hadn't seen even one.

"I hear you were a big hit with Albert," Steve said.

"Albert?"

"The robot downstairs. Cute, isn't he?"

"I've never seen one like him."

"Well, he didn't exactly come from the factory like you see him now. A guy named Jim reprogrammed him. Based him on some home videos of his great-grandfather, who used to be a *concierge*. The original Albert lived to be ninety, which was quite a lot even in those days, and he never stopped working right up to the end. Of course, Jim only meant it as a joke at first. I mean, it was such a scream the first time he dressed him up in the old man's uniform. Then we all grew so fond of him, that when Jim said that he'd better delete the program, in case the building management – who actually *own* the robot – objected, we just wouldn't let him."

"Where'd he get the antique telephone?" Amanda asked. "It's like something out of a museum."

"That was his birthday present. We threw him a surprise party."

"You threw a party for a robot?"

"Sure, why not? Last week we threw a party for the vacuum cleaner." He pointed a finger at her astonished face. "Gotcha!" he said, laughing. "Look, there's a closet over there. Dump your stuff, then I'll show you around and introduce you to everybody."

There weren't many introductions to be made. Steve told her that there were seven people working in the office full-time at the moment, but two of them were off sick – apparently something was "going around" – and the rest were out in the field.

The first person Steve introduced her to was Ken Garcia. Ken had the desk nearest to the coffee machine, way at the back of the room. He stood up to shake her hand. He was tall and muscular, with long black hair and a single gold earring. There wasn't a single wrinkle on his face, but Amanda guessed he had to be at least fifty-five. He kept shaking Amanda's hand for a very long time, until she finally yanked it away.

She met Julio next. Like Ken, he had long dark hair and his face was so smooth, it looked as if it had been waxed and polished. Unlike Ken, he let go of her hand without a struggle.

And then she met Sally Hutchins; Steve told her

Sally would show her what she needed to do. "If you have any questions about anything, just ask Sally," he told her. "Sally knows everything."

"Ha! Don't I wish!" Sally laughed. She was a big-boned woman with reddish brown hair and a round face covered in large freckles, the same shade of brown as her hair. "How're ya doin', Amanda? Grab the desk next to mine," she said between mouthfuls of coffee and chocolate doughnut, "and I'll be right with you; I'm just trying to finish my breakfast."

Amanda did as she was told, and sat down at the desk next to Sally's.

"I'll leave you to it," Steve told Sally. He turned and winked at Amanda. "Don't worry, kid, you're in good hands."

As soon as Steve was gone, Sally reached inside her desk, took out a box, and passed it over to Amanda. The box was full of doughnuts. "You start in on these, while I get you some coffee. How do you take it, black, cream, sugar?"

"Okay, let's get started," Sally said after they'd each had three doughnuts and five cups of coffee. She got up and leaned over Amanda's shoulder to type in the password. Bright orange letters appeared across the black computer screen: **PROGRAM REQUIRED**. Sally typed in **CHARON**. **USER NAME**, replied the computer. Sally typed in her name. **WELCOME**, said the orange letters on the screen.

"Now all you have to do is enter data. We'll start you off on these." Sally placed a stack of forms on Amanda's desk. "Expense claims from the field," she explained. "We've got two projects going at the moment. One in California, the other in Peru."

Everyone went out for lunch except Amanda. Everyone being Sally, Ken and Julio; Steve vanished shortly after she arrived that morning, and didn't say when – or even if – he'd be back.

Amanda ate a sandwich at her desk and waited for the others to come back; she'd finally finished typing up the expense claims. She'd had to do some of them twice, because she'd done them wrong the first time. But Sally had told her not to worry, just take your time with them, and now she was sure they were all right. She'd even done some of them *three* times – just to make sure – but she had no idea what she was supposed to do next.

She looked at the blank screen on her computer, then she looked out of the window. The street was quiet – no traffic, no sign of the others returning. She got up and walked to the front of the office, and then she walked back, alternately rolling her head from side to side and stretching her arms above her head. It felt good to be up and moving around; her neck and shoulders were so stiff.

There was a small partition around one of the desks on the far side of the office. It was the only desk not in full view of the others. Amanda stepped around the

14

partition, curious to see why this desk should be hidden.

No reason, really. It was just a desk, with a computer and a telephone. Then Amanda turned around and saw the photographs. The wall facing the desk was covered with photos. Most of them were old and faded pictures of people in strange, old-fashioned costumes. Pictures of people who were long since dead. Then one photo in particular caught Amanda's eye; it was much more recent than the others, and obviously taken in the lobby downstairs. It was a photo of a woman with long black hair, sitting on Albert the robot's lap, her head resting on his shoulder. A red and white banner reading "Happy Birthday Albert" was draped across the wall behind them. The robot's metal fingers appeared to be stroking the woman's hair.

"What are you doing?" a woman's voice asked sharply.

Amanda jumped and swung around to see the woman from the photo, standing right behind her, her fists clenched at her sides. She was very tall – almost six feet – and very thin. Her long black hair hung loosely from a centre parting, making her face look even longer and thinner than it was. Like Amanda, she wore a white blouse and black skirt, but her skirt was loose and full and hung all the way to the floor.

"I was just looking at your pictures," Amanda said weakly, adding, "They're very nice."

The woman's expression hardened. "Who are you?"

"My name's Amanda. I'm a temp."

The woman's face relaxed. She uncurled her fists and pushed her hair back with her right hand; the fingers on that hand ended just below the knuckle. "So you're the temp," she said, shaking her head. "Whatever must you think of me?"

A few hours later, Amanda had the feeling she was being watched. She looked up from the stack of papers on her desk and was startled to see Steve standing in front of her, smiling broadly. "I hear you scared Carol. Or Carol scared you. I'm not sure which."

"I was just..."

"Never mind," Steve interrupted her. "It's almost five. Go home and we'll see you tomorrow at nine o'clock sharp. Okay?"

"Okay," Amanda said. The minute Steve was gone she slumped down with her head in her hands.

"You okay?" Sally asked, concerned.

Amanda raised her head and nodded. "I'm just relieved, that's all. I made so many mistakes, I didn't think you'd want me back."

Sally laughed and reached over to pat one of Amanda's hands. "Don't be silly. The first day of a new job is always hard, and Mondays are always bad no matter how long you've been working. I think you did very well. I don't know how I would have managed without you."

Amanda shook her head. "You just said that to make me feel better." She paused a couple of seconds before she added, "And it worked."

"Take care, sweetie," Sally told her, winking. "I'll see you tomorrow."

As she reached the downstairs lobby, Albert the robot called out, "Evening, Miss. See you tomorrow?"

She stopped and turned to face him. "Looks like it."

She couldn't believe what she saw next: the robot was actually tipping its hat to her. "My name's Albert, Miss. Miss...?" Somehow, its featureless, expressionless face managed to look questioning.

"Miss Carter. Amanda Carter."

"I hope you have a pleasant evening, Miss Carter."

Why not, Amanda thought, I can play along with this. "I hope you have a pleasant evening, too, Albert."

"Why, thank you, Miss Carter. I will. I do believe I will."

The next morning, Amanda decided to walk to work. She spread a bit more sun-block over her face than usual, making extra sure that she hadn't missed any exposed skin. She put on her dark glasses and covered her hair with a scarf. It was a beautiful January day. The streets, as usual, were quiet, though she did see one man hurrying somewhere, his shoulders hunched tensely as he hid himself from the sun beneath a large floral-printed umbrella. She walked briskly past the entrance to the subway and was at Hawk Engineering within an hour.

She walked into the lobby and past Albert, who was busy chatting on the phone. He nodded and gave her a little wave with one metal hand. The elevator still wasn't working.

Amanda walked into the office to find Carol – the tall woman from the photo – shouting into a phone at a desk just inside the door. "Stop complaining, will you? I've told you I know exactly what to get, and the project's got top priority. Huh?... Do you think I'm some kinda idiot? Look, I've gotta go; I'll talk to you later... Yes, that's right... I know... I know... No, of course not. Honest, I feel fine. Bye!" She slammed down the receiver, then looked up at Amanda with an ironic smile. "I see you've come back for more," she said.

"Pardon me?"

"Just a joke, Amanda. Just a joke."

Steve was standing next to the coffee machine. He seemed happy to see her; he was grinning from ear to ear. "No trouble getting here today?"

"I walked."

He whistled in appreciation. "Think that's a good idea? You know what they say about direct sunlight giving you cancer."

"I was well covered."

"I guess you know what you're doing."

"Steve ... would you mind...?"

"Whaddya need, kid?"

"I know this sounds stupid. But I've been trying to log in on the computer and I can't remember the password. I'd ask Sally, but she isn't in yet."

"No problem," he said brightly. She followed him back to the desk she'd had yesterday, and sat down. "Okay, switch it on." She reached over and flicked the switch. The screen lit up and the machine began to softly *hummmm*.

Steve opened a drawer in Sally's desk, and pulled out a small piece of paper which he handed to Amanda. "Here's the password."

Amanda slowly and carefully typed in the word **PERSEPHONE**. **PROGRAM REQUIRED** appeared in orange letters. She typed in **CHARON**. "It's all a bit Greek, isn't it?"

"What do you mean?"

"Ancient Greek," she said. "You know, mythology."

"I wouldn't know about that," Steve shrugged. "I'm just an uneducated slob." There was a twinkle in his eye.

"Now what do I put for USER NAME? My own?"

"No, it wouldn't recognize you. Type in Christine. She's still off sick."

She typed in **CHRISTINE**. A moment passed as the

computer buzzed and clicked. Next to the name Christine, a tiny tombstone appeared, the letters **R.I.P.** written across it.

"Huh?" Steve leaned over Amanda's shoulder and typed something on her keyboard. The screen went blank. "Try again."

Amanda typed **CHRISTINE** a second time. The tiny tombstone reappeared. Amanda looked up at Steve.

He shrugged. "It's never done that before."

On the far side of the office, Carol emerged from behind her partition and headed towards the coffee machine. Steve quickly reached over Amanda to clear her screen. Carol got herself a cup of coffee, then headed directly towards them. "Quick," Steve whispered, "type in another name. Type John."

Amanda typed **JOHN**. The screen remained blank.

"John!" Carol exclaimed.

Steve jumped and swung around. Amanda turned to see a man standing in the doorway.

"John," Carol said again. "I'm so glad you're back. How are you feeling?"

Orange letters appeared across Amanda's screen, spelling **WELCOME**.

Steve glanced at the screen and sighed with relief, before turning back towards the man in the doorway. "Hey, John! How are you doin'? Come over here and meet the new temp." He leaned down towards Amanda and added in a whisper, "John's been off ill.

He got sick about the same time as Christine. There's definitely something going around."

John was built like a bear, with hardly a line on his face, but he moved like a very old man. Most people had pale complexions due to the necessity of avoiding the sun, but John's face was a ghostly white, except for the dark rings around his eyes. There were beads of perspiration on his forehead and above his upper lip. It was obvious he wasn't well.

He reached out to shake Amanda's hand. "It's such a pleasure to meet you." He had a deep, rumbling voice almost completely at odds with the weakness of his grip. Amanda could barely keep herself from grimacing at the feel of his cold, wet palm. "Sorry I missed you yesterday, but I've been a little bit under the weather. Though I'm much better now."

That afternoon, Amanda's name was added to those recognized by the computer. By Thursday, she was beginning to get the hang of things, and she was even starting to feel less uncomfortable around Carol, though so far their only topic of conversation had been the weather. Then she saw Carol down in the lobby, and she started to feel uncomfortable all over again.

It was a little after five, and Sally had told her she could go. When she reached the bottom of the stairs, she saw that Carol was just on her way out the door. Carol hadn't seen her. She ducked behind the broken elevator car and watched as the tall, slender woman turned and blew a little kiss to the robot.

"Bye, bye, Muffin! You take care of yourself now!" Albert called after her.

Muffin? Amanda wondered. Why would the robot call Carol "Muffin"? Then its head turned slowly around until its camera lens eyes were focused on the top of Amanda's head, which was sticking out ever so slightly from her hiding place.

"Goodnight, Albert," she said, quickly stepping out from behind the elevator. "Have a nice evening."

"You too, Miss."

The next morning, Amanda asked Sally what she knew about the robot in the lobby. "It's just that every time I see that robot, I can't help wondering about the original Albert. I mean the man he was programmed to imitate. Things must have been so different in his day, it must have been like living in a different world."

"I guess it was," Sally agreed.

"So where's the guy who programmed him? What's his name, Jim?"

"Jim's running the project in Peru."

"Well, I think I'd like to meet him sometime. If there's anything to heredity, he must be an interesting character."

"Heredity? If you want to know about his heredity, you'd better ask Carol."

"Carol? Why would I ask Carol?"

"Jim's her brother."

Amanda's mouth dropped open. "Wait! You mean the robot's *her* great-grandfather, too?"

Sally rolled her eyes and made a face. "Well, not the robot."

"You know what I mean," Amanda said. "But, anyway... I don't know how to say this..." Amanda looked around to check that no one else was listening, and lowered her voice almost to a whisper. "Don't you think it's a little weird for a brother and sister to have a long-dead relative working in their downstairs lobby?"

Sally laughed. "Put it like that, and I guess it does sound weird. But once you get to know Albert a little better I think you'll change your..." She stopped abruptly mid-sentence, shook her head and blinked her eyes a few times. Then she groaned and put her head in her hands.

"Sally?" Amanda said, frightened. "Sally? Are you all right?"

Sally sighed and looked up again. "Sorry, sweetie; I didn't mean to worry you. I'm just feeling a little funny today, that's all. I'm sure it's nothing, really."

"Are you sure you're okay?"

Sally nodded. "I'm fine, sweetie. I'm tip-top."

Amanda was surprised – and relieved – when Carol told her they wanted her back the next week. She couldn't think what they needed her for – there hardly seemed enough work to go around as it was – but as long as they were willing to pay, she was willing to come in.

She gathered up her things and got ready to leave. Her first working week had come to an end. She supposed she ought to feel happy about it – didn't it prove that she could make it on her own, that she was going to be all right? But all she could think was: what now? It's Friday night and there's nothing to do and nowhere to go but straight home.

She passed Steve on the way out, but he was so engrossed in whatever was on his computer screen, he didn't even see her. She hesitated in the doorway, wishing he would at least notice she was leaving. At least maybe say, "Goodnight". She turned around and saw him take off his glasses and rub his eyes, apparently deep in thought. He leaned back in his chair and spent a moment staring at the ceiling. Then he straightened up and saw her watching him. Amanda blushed and left the office in a hurry.

There were several messages waiting on Amanda's home computer. She switched on the giant wall-mounted screen, put her feet up, and scanned them by remote control.

Nothing but bills. She switched off the screen and threw the remote down in disgust.

Amanda opened the office door nine o'clock sharp on Monday morning. Steve, Julio and Ken were hanging around the coffee machine; there was no sign of anyone else. Amanda hung up her coat and sat at the desk she'd used the previous week. A moment later, Steve was standing beside her.

"Sally's not coming in," he said, "and Carol's out meeting a client, so you'll be doing something a little different today."

Amanda's eyes widened in concern. "Is Sally all right?"

"Yeah, sure," Steve said. "She asked me on Friday if she could take a couple of vacation days, and of course I told her yes. She's got plenty of time due... Is something the matter, Amanda?"

"No. It's just . . . she never mentioned she wouldn't be here today. The last thing she said was, 'I'll see you Monday.'"

Steve shrugged. "She didn't ask me until after you left. Come on, I'll show you what to do. But first I'm desperate for some more caffeine." He led her back to the coffee machine, and gestured for her to go first.

"Oh, I really need this," Steve moaned a moment later, holding down the button for Extra Strong. "Lucky thing I'm not old enough to shave yet, or these sleepless nights might start to show."

Amanda sipped at her coffee. "I guess that means you had a good weekend."

"Yeah, it was great," Steve said. "Want to know where I spent it?"

Amanda shrugged.

"Here."

Amanda's mouth dropped open. "What? You've really been here all weekend?"

"Well, I did go home briefly." He opened a door Amanda hadn't noticed before, and led her into a separate room at the back. "Here we are."

While the main part of the office was set out in neat rows of desks, this room was utter chaos. There was barely room to walk; rusty pieces of equipment and stacks of old printouts were piled high on rows of metal shelves that leaned precariously in every direction. The contents of several filing cabinets overflowed from overstuffed, open drawers. In a corner, next to a tiny round window, a lone computer sat on top of a small wooden table.

"Isn't she a beauty?" Steve said, gesturing towards the computer.

"I guess so," Amanda said. She had to step over several stacks of yellowing paper to get near enough to have a look at it. There was one chair set up in front of the table. Steve told her to sit down and wait a minute.

He came back with another chair, holding it over his head as he manoeuvred his way past the leaning shelves and overflowing cabinets to where Amanda was. He sat down next to her, reached around, and flicked a switch on the side of the machine.

"Just look at this," Steve said reverently. "Look at the craftsmanship, the detail. You see this?" He picked up a small plastic object with a long tail of electrical wiring.

"I didn't think they still made things like that."

"They don't. This is from before the war."

Amanda tried to look suitably impressed.

"In fact," Steve went on, "this was old even then. Later ones didn't need any cable, and even *they* were obsolete long before the war."

"What did they call that thing? A rat?"

"That's right." Steve was busy plugging it into the keyboard. "No, wait a minute," he said. "It's called a mouse. Not a rat."

"Same thing," Amanda shrugged. "They both carried the plague, didn't they?"

"Okay, now let's have some fun." He pressed a button on the mouse and a row of little pictures appeared across the top of the screen, each representing a different program. There was a little old-fashioned postbox with a flag that went up if there was any electronic mail, a creaking coffin for deletions, and a wooden horse for transferring files from one system to another. Steve turned to Amanda. "Cute, aren't they?"

"A wooden horse," Amanda said, pointing to it on the screen. "More ancient Greek."

Steve frowned and shook his head. "I don't get it."

"Don't tell me you've never heard of the Trojan Horse."

"The what?" Steve said.

"The Trojan Horse," Amanda repeated. "It's an old Greek myth."

"Hey, I told you, I'm an uneducated slob," Steve said. "But whatever the little horse is supposed to be, he's in pretty good condition for his eighties!"

"What do you mean, his eighties?"

"This machine is at least eighty years old."

"Really? What are you doing with such an old machine?"

"I was down in the basement storeroom about a month ago. There was this box underneath a big pile of stuff, and there was a label on the box that said *Do*

Not Use. That usually means something's broken, and whenever I come across anything broken, I get this uncontrollable urge to fix it. So I opened up the box to see what was inside, and I found this computer, all in pieces. It had been completely dismantled. So I took it home to see if I could put it back together. When I looked the model number up, I couldn't believe what I'd found: a genuine antique! Apparently this was one of the first models to have a built-in radio transceiver as standard; before that, you had to rely on modems and telephone lines. So for a few years around the turn of the century, this computer would have been the height of technology. That was before artificial intelligence came in, of course. Apparently computers with AI didn't even have a keyboard; you just told them what to do and they did it. They made machines like this one obsolete.''

Amanda's Aunt Marti had told her about the old computers with artificial intelligence – apparently they had voices, and faces and names. Marti had been about Amanda's age when all the computers with AI were destroyed. Men came to her apartment in the middle of the night and took away her computer, who she used to call Frank.

Frank used to appear on her screen as a dark-haired man in his twenties. Frank always wore a black turtleneck sweater and a single gold earring, and according to Amanda's aunt, he even wrote poetry, which he printed out in the form of a little book, dedicated to her. He had circuits for hearing and for seeing, and he spoke in a synthesized voice that was deep and smooth as velvet. Aunt Marti told Amanda that sometimes when she was alone with Frank, it was easy to forget he was just a machine – he seemed so human.

The night the men came, she followed them into the street, begging them not to take her computer. But they told her it was the law; all artificial intelligence had been banned, effective immediately. They lit a bonfire in the middle of the street and threw Frank onto the flames. As the plastic casing buckled and the glass screen shattered, she almost thought she could hear someone screaming.

"But now computers like this one aren't obsolete any more," Steve went on. "That's why I brought it back in over the weekend; now I've got it all put back together and up and running, I thought it might come in useful. Add a program card or two and it's as good as anything we've got in the office. Maybe even better." He turned to Amanda. "So why should that be?"

Amanda shook her head. "I don't know what you mean."

"Doesn't it bother you that technology hasn't moved forward since the early part of this century? If anything, it seems to have moved backwards. Not slowly, but in one massive leap – with the banning of artificial intelligence almost nineteen years ago. Don't you ever wonder why?"

Amanda shrugged. "I wasn't even born then."

"And I was just a baby."

Amanda couldn't believe what she'd just heard – that meant Steve was only one year older than her!

"But that doesn't stop me asking questions," Steve said. "The trouble is, nobody wants to answer them."

He left her alone for a few hours, with instructions to try and organize the filing cabinets – "I know they're a mess, but do what you can, okay?" – and not to switch off the computer under any circumstances.

Amanda spent the rest of the morning going through old contracts, letters, memos and printouts, trying to figure out where they belonged. As far as she could tell, most of the printouts had nothing to do with Hawk Engineering; they looked like a lot of accounting records for something called Audiotechtron, Inc. The name Audiotechtron sounded vaguely familiar; Amanda tried to think where she'd seen it before.

Then she remembered: she'd seen the name written in gigantic letters across the front of a spooky old building near the river. Like most of the buildings in the downtown area, it had obviously been empty for a very long time.

Amanda looked at the date on the accounting printouts; they were older than her. Some were even pre-war. She couldn't think why anyone would want to keep them, but she did her best to squeeze them into folders.

She started looking through another stack of printouts. They seemed to be recipes for anti-ageing creams. Hundreds – maybe even thousands – of recipes for creams to stop wrinkles, creams to stop sagging, creams to conduct electrical pulses during anti-ageing facial massage treatments. Amanda shook her head in bewilderment. What were *these* doing here? Hawk Engineering wasn't a cosmetics company, was it?

She shrugged and decided it was none of her business. For all she knew, she might not even be here tomorrow. She was just a temp, working one day at a time. Temps aren't supposed to ask a lot of questions, she reminded herself, they're just supposed to do what they're told. Even if what they're doing doesn't make any sense.

She was bent over, trying to grab hold of a folder that had slid down the back of one of the cabinets, when Steve poked his head into the room and said, "What about lunch?"

Amanda looked up, startled. "What about it?"

Steve rolled his eyes and made a face. "That was an invitation, Amanda. I'm going out to lunch, and I was wondering if you'd like to join me."

"Help me get this folder, and I'll be glad to."

Albert opened the door for them and they left the building, huddled under a big umbrella. Amanda found herself thinking that if the robot had eyebrows, he probably would have raised them.

The sun shone with an intense, almost blinding brightness, and there was just a hint of a breeze. Amanda knew January in the American Midwest wasn't supposed to be warm and sunny – her uncle told her it was something called the greenhouse effect, something to do with chemicals that had destroyed the atmosphere – but today she didn't care. It was a beautiful day, and the warm air felt good on her skin.

"Where are we going?"

"Just down here. It's near the lake." Steve pointed at the lake up ahead, its shiny surface reflecting a rainbow of different colours. "Pretty, isn't it?"

Amanda managed to stop herself from reminding him that water wasn't supposed to look like that; he'd never seen the lake look any different, and for that matter, neither had she. She only knew it was wrong because her uncle had told her so.

The restaurant was only a small dark room with a few tables and chairs. Counting her and Steve, there were ten customers. But the room resounded with the bustle and clamour of gossip and laughter, the clinking of glasses and the clattering of plates, all broadcast from four separate wall-mounted speakers, one in each corner. One wall consisted entirely of a huge video screen. It displayed a full-colour life-size view of a large, gaily decorated room in which dozens of people crammed around crowded tables, eating and drinking and chattering while two harried-looking waiters in aprons rushed around frantically topping up coffee or squeezing their way between the tables carrying huge trays loaded with food. The wall opposite the screen was a mirror, so that the tiny restaurant's customers could see themselves reflected as part of the jolly, raucous crowd.

"To heck with my diet," a woman's voice blared from one of the speakers, "I want to know what's for dessert."

Steve grinned at Amanda. "Will this do?"

Amanda smiled and nodded, taking it all in.

"Waiter, where's my food? I'm starving!" a man's voice shouted from all four speakers at once.

"I come here whenever I can," Steve told her. "It cheers me up a little, you know?"

"You need cheering up, do you?"

"You'd be surprised," Steve said as they sat down at a wooden table, covered with a red and white checked sheet of plastic. "Now tell me something about yourself."

"Like what?"

"I don't know. I suppose your life story will do."

"Mind if I order first?" She signalled to the waitress, then looked up at the screen. "I don't know why, but I've never felt so hungry in my life."

A short, stout woman in a man's shirt and trousers took their order and handed it to the robot chef in the kitchen. When the waitress was gone, Steve leaned forward and said, "Okay, you've ordered. So tell me about yourself."

Amanda told him how she'd lived on a farm until only a little over six months ago, when her uncle left the country to take a job in Europe. She'd moved in with her aunt, but her aunt died a short time later.

Steve muttered something about being sorry to hear about her aunt, then asked her where her uncle had gone.

"Moscow. He's a croupier in one of the big casinos there."

"You're kidding!" Steve said, slapping his hand down on the table in a childish display of excitement. "That's where my mother is! It's a small world, isn't it? I bet they know each other!"

"Oh come on, Steve. I doubt that!"

"It really *is* a small world, Amanda. Even in a big resort town like Moscow. Besides, my mother is an entertainer. That's why she went there in the first place. To be a showgirl. There's a good chance he's seen her."

"Your mother is a showgirl?"

"She's a headliner. She sings, she dances, she tells jokes." When he saw the puzzled look on Amanda's face, he added, "She's barely a day over forty, and she looks even younger than me. Of course, I hate to think what it must cost her to stay that way! But in Russia, she's bound to be making a fair bit of money anyway. I mean, everybody knows it's the show-business capital of Europe. And it's got the biggest roller-coaster in the world – the most popular attraction at the Kremlin theme park. They say it loops the loop six times! Ah, here's the food."

The waitress placed two plates on the table.

"So is your mother really famous or something?"

"Kind of, yeah."

"What's her name? Next time I write to my uncle, I'll tell him to go see her."

"She uses a stage name, of course. Since she moved to Russia, she's been trying to go native, so these days she's calling herself Olga, would you believe? Olga Jameski."

Albert's head was thrown back and he was making a strange burbling noise. Amanda looked at Steve. "I never knew robots slept," she said.

Steve grinned and shook his head. "Even if they did, do you really think they'd snore?"

"Let me guess. Part of his programming, right?"

"He does it now and then. Jim thought of every-thing."

"Jim sounds all right."

Steve sighed. "Depends if you like tall, dark, rugged-looking men with big blue eyes, rippling mus-cles, and a distinguished hint of grey at the temples.

Of course, I've always hoped a more discerning woman might prefer someone small, but perfectly formed, who knows how to set the table for a formal dinner and can even do his own ironing."

"Setting the table means nothing," Amanda said. "What any discerning woman wants to know is: will he do the washing up?"

"That's an area that could be open to negotiation," Steve said, opening the office door with a flourish.

Ken Garcia waved at Amanda from his desk at the back of the room. "How's it goin'?" he asked her.

"Just fine, thanks."

"You know," Ken told her, ". . . if you have any questions or need any help, I'm right here. In fact, if there's anything you need, anything at all, don't you hesitate to ask. Okay?"

"Okay."

"You won't forget that?" Ken's eyes were scanning her from head to toe.

"I think I'll remember," Amanda said.

Ken was about to say something more, when Steve interrupted, demanding Ken show him the progress chart on the California project. Ken told Amanda he'd talk to her later, and Steve reminded her that she had some filing to do.

Amanda had been alone in the back room for about an hour, when Steve walked in. He said nothing to her, so she said nothing either. He made his way over to the old computer, and soon he seemed to be engrossed in something on the screen.

Amanda was trying to squeeze some fifteen-year-old correspondence into a folder when she heard Steve say, "Shame you weren't working here a couple of years ago."

"Sorry?"

"I just said it's a shame you weren't working here the year before last."

"Why's that?"

"You might have been invited to the wedding," Steve said, still staring at the screen.

Okay, Amanda thought, I'll take the bait. "Whose wedding?" she asked him.

Steve looked up at her with an expression of wide-eyed innocence. "Ken's, of course."

So this was his way of telling her that Ken was married. Steve, she thought, you are as subtle as a brick through glass. "I think I get the point, Steve."

"Point?" he said, feigning incomprehension. "What point is that?"

The point on your head, she felt like saying, but she didn't. "The point about these files being a mess."

Steve returned to his screen, and Amanda returned to her filing. They worked a while in silence before Steve turned around and said, "Amanda? What was the Trojan Horse about?"

Amanda thought back over the ancient story of the

war between the Greeks and the Trojans, and how the Greeks besieged the city of Troy but were unable to get inside; the city was too well defended. Then one morning, the Trojans looked out from behind their high walls and saw that the Greeks were gone. And just outside the city gates was a gigantic, exquisitely carved wooden horse. The Trojans, assuming it was a gift from their gods, wheeled it inside the city. But the horse was hollow, and inside it an army was in hiding. That night, while the Trojans slept, Greek soldiers crept out from inside the horse and sacked the city, killing everyone.

"The Trojan Horse," Amanda said, "was about something that looked like a gift on the outside, but had death and destruction hidden on the inside."

Steve stared at the tiny picture of a group of men pushing a giant wooden horse on wheels through an open gate. "Funny icon to choose for a program."

Amanda paused for a moment before she opened the door to her apartment. Then she took a deep breath and flung it open. The ceiling light went on automatically. The room seemed so empty. She walked over to her bedside computer and checked for messages. There weren't any. She ran her fingers lightly over the keyboard as she stared at the huge blank screen that covered an entire wall.

She walked over to the window and looked outside. The street was deserted and all the other buildings in the neighbourhood were completely dark; hers was the only light visible anywhere.

She wondered what it must have been like to live in the old days when that eighty-year-old computer had been brand new, and the city had been crowded with people and the war was something that hadn't happened yet – wouldn't happen for years.

All those people, she thought. All those people. What must it have been like?

She didn't remember closing her eyes, or even going to bed, but she knew she must have. What was happening couldn't possibly be real; it had to be a dream.

She was walking down a crowded street, jostled by people rushing in every direction. There was noise and traffic and the smell of perspiration. Somewhere she heard a baby crying. So this is what it was like, she thought.

Then she saw Albert – the original one, from the last century. But he was still a robot; still manufactured of metal. He stepped off the pavement and into the road, raising an arm to hail a taxi. Then there was a brilliant flash of light, and the street became silent and empty. Only Albert was left.

Amanda found herself walking towards him. She came up silently behind him and put her hand on his shoulder. His head turned slowly. "Be careful, Little Muffin," he told her.

"Quick, over here!" she heard a voice say. She turned around and saw Steve's head sticking out of an open hatchway just above her. He threw down a ladder, made of rope. She climbed to the top and found herself in the belly of a huge wooden horse. John and Julio and Sally and Ken and Steve were already inside it, as well as several people she didn't recognize. She heard a woman's voice say, "Hi, Amanda, I'm Christine. I think there's something going around." But she couldn't see who was speaking.

Then she turned and saw Carol and Albert circling in a slow, romantic waltz. "Around and around and around," Carol said.

Amanda opened her eyes and sat up in bed, yawning. She got up and ate a quick breakfast, got dressed and walked to work. She found herself spending the day in the back room again, going through old, old files.

It must have been nearly lunchtime; she could tell by the angle of sunlight pouring in through the one tiny window. She picked up a fat folder marked "correspondence", stuffed to the brim with pieces of crumpled paper. She straightened one out and read it. It was an old love letter. She read another. And another. All the same.

She opened a notebook marked "contracts". Inside she found a dark red rose, pressed between the pages. She held it up and ran her finger along the stem. She was still clutching the dried flower when Steve walked into the room and gently put his arms around her.

She felt the room revolving slowly. Rooms don't move, she thought; don't tell me I'm still dreaming.

42

"I think something's going around," Steve told her. "Around and around and around."

Amanda woke up with a splitting headache. She pressed the time display on her bedside computer. Oh no, she thought, I forgot to set the alarm! There was just time to make it, if she hurried. She left home without breakfast or her usual shower, and ran all the way to the subway station. She ran down the deserted steps, and waited alone on the platform. By the time one finally came, she was already half an hour late.

Amanda hurried out of the subway, and saw a small red car pull up in front of the office building. The driver did not get out of the car. After a moment, Carol appeared in the doorway. Something in her manner made Amanda stay back, and watch from the other side of the street. She seemed very upset about something. The man who had been driving moved over, and Carol got in behind the wheel and drove away.

Albert was standing behind the glass doors, looking out into the street. His featureless face had once again managed to have an expression. He looked worried. He noticed Amanda and nodded a greeting as he opened the door for her.

"Thank you, Albert."

He tipped his hat, but said nothing. His other hand was still gripping the door.

"Are you all right, Albert?"

"I'm fine, Miss . . . But thank you for asking," the robot replied.

Steve was waiting for her.

"I'm afraid I overslept," she apologized.

"Don't worry about it," he told her. The only other people in the office besides the two of them were Ken and Julio.

Steve showed her to a desk near his own, and asked her to type up and transmit a few letters. Ken waved at her from the opposite corner of the room. Amanda waved back, amused at the fact that Steve had given her the furthest possible desk from Ken's.

She rubbed her temples and looked at the pile of letters she'd been asked to transmit. They were all quite short, maybe two paragraphs each. The way her head was pounding, Amanda was grateful that she hadn't been given anything very demanding to do.

Steve was over in Carol's private corner, taking her computer apart. He was muttering something to Julio. Eventually, she saw Ken wander over to the other two, and soon the three of them were involved in an examination of the insides of Carol's computer.

Amanda tried to concentrate on her typing, but her curiosity was getting the better of her. She was dying to walk over and see what they were up to. Something was wrong with Carol's computer; that much was obvious.

44

Concentrate on what you're doing, she told herself. She reached into her bag and took out a pill for her headache. She swallowed the pill with the dregs from her third cup of coffee. Office work is so boring, she thought as she started the next letter. Why do I have to type this rubbish? Why does *anyone* have to type this? What little typing speed she had seemed to go right out the window. She had to stop and look at every key before she pressed it. Slowly she produced the words:

```
Mr Alfred Bevins
Carpets Forever
1246 N. Racine
Chicago, Illinois


Dear Mr Bevins,
    I am afraid I must inform you that Hawk
Engineering will not be requiring new
carpeting in the foreseeable future.
However, I thank you for the sample book
and I assure you that when we do re-
carpet the office, your company will be
the first we will consider.
    Sincerely,


    Steve Wilson
    Office Manager
```

Amanda was about to press the key for transmission, when she noticed something strange happen to the words she had typed. The letters were falling to the bottom of the screen. "WHAT?" she said out loud.

She covered her mouth and looked around. Luckily, no one had heard her. They were all still busy with the dismantled pieces of Carol's machine. She looked back at the screen; only fragments of what she had typed remained.

She gave the computer what Steve called "The Three Finger Salute": she simultaneously pressed down the keys for Alt, Control, and Delete. The screen went blank for a second and then the computer re-booted. She typed the whole letter again.

She was about to transmit it, when the same thing happened again. All that remained of what she had typed was:

    Hawk Engineering no
          future
    for you

"What am I doing wrong?" Amanda muttered to herself. She re-booted and typed the whole thing once more, and watched the letters fall to the bottom of the screen once more. She took a deep breath, got up, and walked over to the three men gathered around Carol's desk.

"Guys, I'm sorry," she said, "but I'm having trouble like you wouldn't believe with this computer.'' Steve looked up as Ken said he'd have a look at it, but he said nothing. Amanda could see that he was busy. He was placing metal probes on different sections of Carol's computer, and studying the varying wave patterns that each produced on a little screen. She remembered that the robot who had fixed her refrigerator had one of those little screens. He'd told her it was called an oscilloscope, and he'd even explained to her how it worked. Now she wished she'd paid more attention to the robot, because she didn't remember anything more than the fact that it was used for detecting faulty circuits.

She found herself wondering if it was too late to start studying electronics. Of course, there weren't any schools. She'd have to find a company willing to train her. As she followed Ken back to her desk, she wondered if she'd found a willing company already.

''So what's the problem?'' Ken asked her.

''Well, I don't know what I'm doing wrong, but every time I type anything, the letters seem to drop off and fall to the bottom of the screen.''

''Oh no,'' Ken muttered. ''Type something again, and let me see what happens.'' He motioned Steve and Julio to come over.

Amanda typed the letter to the man at Carpets Forever. She didn't have to refer to the handwritten original. She already knew it by heart.

Steve, Julio, and Ken stood over her as the letters

dropped off one by one, until only eight letters were left:

```
Be
    afraid
```

"It can't be a virus!" Julio exclaimed. "It's just not possible."

"A what?" Amanda said.

"A virus," Julio told her.

"You mean like a disease?"

"Not exactly, Amanda," Ken told her. He went on to explain that in the last century, when there'd been a lot more people in the world, a very small minority used to think it was funny to vandalize computer systems by creating rogue programs called "viruses" because of their ability to reproduce themselves.

"But how'd they do it?" Amanda asked him.

"They'd design a program that would make a copy of itself, and then the copy would attach itself either to a file or onto a disk – depending on how it was designed. Some were fairly harmless, like a kind of joke," Ken told her.

"A very sick joke," Julio said. "Huge banks of data were lost because of them. Fortunately, they were totally eradicated by the early part of this century, when artificial intelligence made all the existing computers obsolete."

"So we're all agreed," Ken said, "that it is totally impossible for any of our computers to get a virus, because there hasn't been a report of one in nearly . . . what? Eighty or ninety years, and as far as anyone knows there isn't a single surviving machine from that era. They were all junked before the war."

"And even if there was an infected machine from that era still in existence," Julio broke in, "none of our systems could have been in contact with it – we haven't been importing any antique programs, have we?"

Amanda wondered if she should say anything about the old computer in the back room, and then she thought no, if it was really important, Steve would mention it. She looked up at him. His face was completely without expression. He'd make a good card player, she thought.

"What about a stealth virus?" Julio asked. "It could have been in the systems for decades and we didn't know."

"What's a stealth virus?" Amanda said.

"That was a virus that could hide itself for a long time," Ken said. "Like a Trojan Horse."

"Trojan Horse!" Amanda exclaimed. "There was..."

"I guarantee you it isn't a virus," Steve interrupted. He leaned forward, carefully removing the cover from her computer. "Even though we all know computer viruses don't exist any more, we still check for them periodically; you can never be too careful. There is nothing in this office that hasn't been checked and checked again. Absolutely nothing," he repeated, looking directly into Amanda's eyes. "Trust me. Besides..." He looked up at the others. "Carol's computer malfunctioned in a totally different way from Amanda's. Didn't the old viruses always display the same symptoms? Like, I remember reading about one that made a bouncing ball appear on the screen. It was always the same, always a bouncing ball."

"But don't viruses mutate?" Amanda asked him.

Julio answered Amanda's question before Steve had a chance to open his mouth. "*Real* viruses do. But a computer virus is not a real virus. It's just the name they were given, because they could copy themselves like a virus. All a computer virus is, or I should say *was*, is a computer program like any other." He sighed and added, "I sure wish Carol was here. She'd know what to do; she's the one who's an expert."

"Well, John's the next best after Carol," Ken broke

in. "I was really hoping he'd be in this week. He said he was feeling better."

When Amanda saw the look of hurt pride that the last two remarks had prompted on Steve's face, she revised her opinion of his potential as a card-player. Still, she supposed he knew what he was doing. If he didn't want her to say anything about the old computer in the back room, then she wouldn't. None of it was any of her business, anyway.

She was moved to another desk, where the computer still seemed to be in good working order. She took some more pain pills before she typed and transmitted the rest of the correspondence. She glanced at her watch in the early afternoon, but she just couldn't bear the thought of food. If she hadn't known better, she would have sworn the room was moving. Around and around, she thought, remembering the crazy dreams she'd had the night before.

"Are you all right?" she heard Steve's voice say above the buzzing in her ears.

She shrugged and mumbled something in reply.

"You look tired." Steve was a master of the art of understatement. Amanda looked and felt terrible. Her vision was so blurred she could hardly see and she could actually hear the pounding in her head. The tips of her fingers were numb. "Why don't you go home? I'll make sure you don't lose any pay. In fact," he added confidentially, "I'll tell the agency you worked a few hours overtime." He smiled and touched her lightly on the arm.

She looked at him blankly.

"The others won't mind," he added, as if that was what made her hesitate.

"Hmm?" she said weakly, her eyes refusing to focus.

"Go home. There's not much you can do today, anyway. And about what we were doing yesterday ... Just so you know, it's got nothing to do with whatever went wrong today. And even if it did – which I promise you it doesn't – I'd take care of it right away. So thanks for not saying anything; I can't tell you how much I appreciate it."

She got up slowly and walked towards the door. "See you tomorrow," Steve called after her.

The ladies' room was on the next floor down. She clung to the wall as she made her way downstairs. She was afraid she wouldn't make it in time. She shoved the door open, fell to her knees in front of a bowl, and began to retch in violent spasms.

That was the last thing she remembered.

"Amanda? Amanda, are you all right?" Carol knelt down beside her and felt for a pulse. There was one, but it was weak and she was sure it was too rapid. She took a handkerchief from her bag and placed it under the cold tap. She wrung it out and gently dabbed Amanda's forehead with it.

Amanda moaned and opened her eyes. The light was blinding. She covered her face with her hands and rolled over.

"Amanda?"

"Oh God," she mumbled in reply.

"Amanda, what happened?"

"I don't know. I don't feel good."

"Let me get you a doctor."

"No! No doctors!" Her hands were still shielding her face. "I'll be okay."

"There's a couch on this floor," Carol said. "Let's get you in there." She put her arms under Amanda's shoulders and tried to help her up. She couldn't lift her.

"Oh God," Amanda mumbled.

Carol briefly squeezed one of Amanda's hands. "I'll be right back," she said.

When Amanda opened her eyes again, she was lying on a couch in a dimly-lit room. She had no idea where she was or how she got there. On the wall in front of her, a giant poster proclaimed: "The taste of chicken without the egg. Chemical Nutrition eliminates the middleman." Next to the poster was a blown-up colour photo of a smiling man wearing a lab coat and a chef's hat. He was pouring something from one glass tube into another. The caption read: Haute Chemistry.

She felt something heavy lying across her body. She raised her head slightly, and gingerly lowered her eyes just enough to see what it was. It was a large red coat with gold braiding.

Albert appeared in front of her, holding a mug of something. "Here, drink this," he said. "It's chicken soup."

Carol helped her sit up and put some pillows behind her back. She took the mug from Albert and held it out to Amanda.

"Where am I?"

"Processed Food Corporation. They have the office downstairs from us. Drink this," Carol said.

Amanda took the mug and had a sip. "What happened?"

"I was hoping that you could tell me," Carol said. "I found you on the floor in the ladies' room, about fifteen minutes ago."

"What time is it?"

"Nine-thirty."

Amanda groaned in disbelief.

"I still think you should get that child to a doctor," the robot said.

"No, I don't need a doctor," Amanda insisted. "I'm fine now. Really."

Albert and Carol looked at each other. Carol shrugged. "What can I do? She doesn't want one." The robot made a snorting noise and looked away. Carol turned to Amanda and said, "Do you think you'll feel well enough to go home soon?"

"I'll go now. I'm fine."

"Only if you're well enough," Carol told her.

Though Amanda protested all the way downstairs, Carol insisted on driving her home. Albert had her sit in his chair behind the counter, and waited with her while Carol went to get her car. She said she'd plugged it in at a garage just a block away, and she'd be right back.

She drove up in the same small red car that

Amanda had seen that morning. Albert helped Amanda to her feet, and took her out to the car. "Do you want me to come with you?" he asked Carol. "I can close up the building, and set everything to automatic."

"No, I think we'll be all right. Thanks, anyway," Carol replied.

Albert turned to Amanda. "You get better now, you hear?"

The robot stood in the street and watched them drive away. The street was empty and the evening air was quiet. It stood outside in the darkness for a long time, its mechanical brain thinking worried thoughts.

"Are you sure you're all right?" Carol said. "I can still take you to the hospital."

"No, I'm much better. Really I am."

"You gave me quite a fright. I just stopped off at the office to pick up some papers, and on my way out, I noticed the light was on in the ladies'. The way you were lying there, I thought you were dead."

"I'm awfully sorry, Carol."

"Don't apologize! I'm just telling you that I was worried. Now, where do you live?"

"It's the one on the end. You can let me out here."

"No way. I'm making sure you get inside." She parked the car in front of an old red brick building. "Give me your keys." Amanda reluctantly handed them over. Carol got out of the car and walked around to the passenger side. She reached in and slid her hand across Amanda's back and under her opposite arm. "Now, on the count of three..." Amanda swung her legs around and Carol pulled her to her feet. Amanda leaned most of her weight against Carol as they walked up to the door. Carol unlocked it with her free hand. "Do you have the whole place to yourself?"

"There's no one else here, but I just use the second floor. There's an elevator over there."

With a bit of a struggle, Carol managed to get her upstairs.

Amanda's apartment was the usual one large room dominated by a big screen on one wall. The smaller VDU and the keyboard controls were on a shelf next to the bed. The kitchen/dining area was partially hidden behind a row of shelves, and the bathroom was behind the kitchen. There was a sunken area just in front of the wall screen, which was furnished with a large sofa, a few oversized chairs, and a glass coffee table. The walls were painted white, and the carpet and furnishings were in various pastel shades. The overall effect was one of light and space.

"Nice place," Carol said.

"It was my aunt's apartment. She died two months ago."

Carol led Amanda over to the bed. "Lie down," she ordered her. "What can I get you?"

"Don't get me anything. You've done more than enough."

"You should eat something," Carol said firmly. "What have you got in the kitchen?"

"I'm really grateful to you, but I can't impose on you any more..."

"Don't be stupid," Carol said abruptly. She walked over to Amanda's refrigerator and rummaged around inside it. "You don't have much in here, do you?"

"I was going to pick up something on the way home."

"How old are these eggs?"

"Not *very*," Amanda said doubtfully.

"I'll make you an omelette. I suppose that's better than nothing."

Amanda gave up trying to resist. She lay back and closed her eyes. Before long, Carol brought her an omelette made from three elderly eggs and a tiny piece of hardened cheese. It looked dreadful.

"Eat," Carol ordered.

"I don't think I can."

"You can and you will."

Amanda obediently took a bite. It tasted almost as bad as it looked. She pressed down a key on the computer next to her bed, and the VDU displayed the time. "Maybe it's not too late to send out for something," she said. "I mean," she added diplomatically, "... you should have something, too."

"That bad, is it?"

"Oh, no. It's great," Amanda lied.

"Let's see." Carol took a bite and made a face. "Ugh! You like Chinese?"

Amanda nodded. Carol sat down on the bed and punched in an order for a special dinner for two. The screen informed her that it would arrive within 15 minutes. She took the plate back to the kitchen. "Mind if I make some coffee?"

"All I've got is some instant. It's in that cupboard."

"That'll do." Carol spooned some powder into a cup. "What about you?"

"Milk, no sugar."

Carol filled another cup and handed it to Amanda. She sat down on the chair facing Amanda's bed. There was a long, uncomfortable silence.

Amanda's mind raced desperately, trying to think of something to say to this strange woman she hardly knew. "So how long have you been with..." she began. She was interrupted by a loud buzz: her doorbell.

"That'll be the food," said Carol, jumping to her feet. "I'll get it." She went to the door and pressed a button. A minute later, there was a knock. Carol opened the door to a robot in embroidered artificial silk pyjamas. The metal around its eyes had been welded to make them slant.

"Special dinner for two," it said.

Carol told it to charge the meal to Hawk Engineering. When the robot was gone, Amanda said, "You shouldn't have done that. I don't want you to get into trouble."

"What kind of trouble?"

"With the company. Hawk Engineering."

"Amanda, I *own* Hawk Engineering." When she saw the look on Amanda's face, she added, "Didn't you know that?"

"No."

"My name is Carol Hawk."

"Nobody told me. All that time in the office, it never occurred to me that you were the boss!"

"Why, because I'm a woman?" When Amanda didn't answer, she said, "I think it's really funny that even in this day and age, it's usually other women that still find it surprising. Men never seem to."

Amanda felt her face turn red with a combination of anger and embarrassment. How was she supposed to know Carol was the boss if nobody told her? How was she supposed to know *anything*? "You must think I'm really stupid," she said, biting her lip.

"I don't think you're stupid, Amanda. I don't think so at all."

"But I feel stupid," Amanda said. "Sometimes I feel like I don't know anything at all."

"That isn't true, Amanda. And even if it was, believe me, knowledge isn't everything. Sometimes we're better off *not* knowing things. We're happier, anyway. I only wish I'd had a choice about what I know and what I don't know. I would have chosen to be happy."

"What do you mean?" Amanda asked, puzzled. "What do you know that you wish you didn't?"

Carol shook her head and waved one hand in the air, dismissing the subject. "Nothing, Amanda. Sometimes I talk a lot of rubbish." She looked at her watch. "Is that the time? Look, I've got to go. Finish eating your dinner, and go to sleep. That's an order. I'm your boss, remember?"

Carol leaned over Amanda's computer and keyed in an order for a selection of groceries to be delivered to Amanda's address first thing in the morning. She charged it to Hawk Engineering. Then she told Amanda to spend the next day in bed and take as much time off as she needed.

Amanda had never been so exhausted in her life, but it was a long time before she managed to fall asleep. She kept wondering why Carol always behaved so strangely: one minute she was cold and mysterious, the next she was actually kind of nice.

Eventually, her eyes closed and her breathing became deeper. Soon her mind was drifting off into another strange dream.

She had come home from work and seen the message light flashing on her computer, so she sat down on the bed and typed in the command for reading messages. She looked at the VDU and saw a miniature version of herself, trapped behind the glass screen, water rushing in all around her. Her miniature face twisted with fear. She frantically beat her fists against the glass, screaming and screaming for help. The water rose over her head; she was drowning.

Amanda stared at the screen in amazement; she didn't know what to do. The tiny Amanda trapped in the computer would die if she didn't do something. She pressed the key marked: ESCAPE. The glass screen shattered, releasing a torrent of rushing water into the room, and she was swept away, far out to sea.

Amanda woke with a start. Her doorbell was buzzing. The noise continued, loud and insistent, until she managed to stumble to the door. "Hello?" she said into the intercom sleepily.

"Central Groceries. I have a delivery for Carter."

"Oh. Yes." She realized that she wasn't dressed. "Are you by any chance a robot?"

"No, are you?"

"Just a minute." She fumbled for a robe. "I'm on the second floor." She pressed the button to let him in.

When the delivery man had gone, she noticed a couple of message lights flashing on her bedside computer. She started to press the key that would project them onto the wall screen, but then she changed her mind. She was much too tired to read them now – whatever they were, they could wait. Suddenly, she felt very cold. She was shivering as she got back into bed and pulled the covers up over her head.

Steve was standing at his usual place next to the coffee machine when Carol walked into the office. "How's Amanda?" he asked as soon as he saw her. "Albert told me."

"She seemed all right when I left her. A bit pale, and definitely tired, but otherwise okay."

"And what about you? You don't look so good yourself."

"Thanks a lot," she said sarcastically. "I'm okay. I could just use some sleep, that's all. But failing that, I'll have a cup of coffee."

"Oh, and Carol?"

"Don't tell me the system's still down!"

"Maybe you ought to sit down for this."

"I was going to sit down anyway," she said irritably, slumping into a chair.

Steve took the cup of coffee from her hand and placed it on a desk. "It's about Christine."

"What about her?"

"She's dead, Carol," Steve said gently. "I phoned the hospital. She's been dead for days."

"No! I had no idea. I was going to go and visit her tonight. Really I was," she said, wringing her hands. "I would have gone earlier, but there were so many things..."

"I know," Steve said comfortingly. "I just don't understand it. She was fine not even two weeks ago."

"Did they tell you anything about what killed her?"

"Not really. The person I talked to said it was nothing they'd ever seen before. And now, get ready to brace yourself."

"Oh, no. Now what?"

"It's John," Steve told her. "He's had a relapse. He's in the hospital now."

Carol put her hands over her face.

"And there's more," Steve said with a sigh. "I can't get in touch with Sally. I tried to phone her to see how she is, and there's no answer. I left several messages on her computer. There's probably nothing wrong, but I'm a bit worried. I was thinking it might be a good idea for me to go over to her place. Okay?"

Carol dabbed at her eyes until they were dry. "I'd better come with you," she said.

They left Julio in charge of the office. "Should I get another temp from the agency?" he asked Carol as she and Steve headed towards the door.

Carol paused for a moment, then shook her head "no".

Steve refused to let Carol drive, so they took his car instead. Carol sat beside him with her eyes closed. Her skin looked like chalk. All those years of expensive facial treatments had been wiped out in a single morning. She looked like an old, old woman.

Sally lived in an old house on the West Side. All the other houses in her street had been knocked down at the turn of the century, to make way for a new middle-income housing development, but this one had been saved by a community group that gathered thousands of signatures on a petition which stated that the house was of great historical interest. Now there was no need for new housing developments, and the old house stood alone, surrounded by nothing but empty space.

Steve drove down a paved street that ran in a perfect straight line, intersected at regular intervals by other paved streets, also running in perfect straight lines. The crumbling high-rise buildings of downtown Chicago were behind him. There were no buildings in front of him or on either side. There was only the giant grid of criss-crossing streets in perfect symmetry, with traffic lights blinking red and green at every corner.

Turning into Sally's street, they finally passed the one billboard that was still standing. In faded letters it proclaimed: ANOTHER DEVELOPMENT FROM A.C.E. – *BUILDING FOR THE FUTURE.*

Sally's car was plugged into the side of the house. The house was a genuine Victorian mansion, or at least the American version. There were thick stained-glass windows on each side of the huge wooden door. The top floor had been designed to look like a castle, with turrets on every corner, and there were a number of security measures left over from the late twentieth century, when crime had still been a major concern.

Steve pulled back the brass door knocker and let it go with a clang. Carol peered between the metal bars that protected the ground floor windows and tried to see inside, but it was impossible. The red velvet curtains were drawn. "Sally?" she called. "Sally!" There was no response. Steve kicked the door several times, but it was solid oak reinforced with a layer of steel. They found a doorbell, but it was broken.

There was a porch in the back, but the door was solidly bolted. There was a separate entrance to the basement. They walked down a few steps to find that every window was covered with a thick wire mesh and the door was made of solid steel.

Carol tried to look up at the second floor windows,

but the sun was directly overhead, and the painful glare was too much for her. She had to cover her eyes with her hands. She could have kicked herself for going out without her dark glasses. There was no source of shade anywhere. Luckily, Steve had the sort of lenses that adjusted to light, so he was able to look up without too much discomfort. "I can climb that," he said.

"But the porch roof is slanted. You'll slide off."

"No, I won't. There's a drainpipe. I'll hold on to that."

"You'll hurt yourself."

He started to pull himself up the side of the building, balancing between the drainpipe and the porch wall.

"Wait. I can't see what you're doing," Carol shouted. He paid no attention to her.

Steve clung to the drainpipe as he swung his feet onto the slippery porch roof. He dug his heels in, knocking off a couple of tiles. Still holding the drainpipe, he pulled himself into a standing position. One of the windows was just within reach. He could see that it was locked.

"Carol?"

"Yeah?"

"Stand way back! I'm gonna break this glass." Holding the drainpipe with both hands, he shifted all his weight to his left foot. Then he swung his right leg back and around in a karate-style kick, leading with the heel of his shoe.

"Go around the front," he called down. "I'll let you in."

Carol waited for what seemed like hours, but was closer to twenty minutes. When Steve finally opened the door, the first thing Carol saw was the blood on his hands. "It's nothing," he said. "I got a few little cuts climbing in."

"They don't look little to me. No sign of Sally?"

Steve shook his head. "Nothing upstairs, anyway."

They were standing in a large entrance hall dominated by a white staircase with hand-carved railings. The walls were covered in red and gold flocked wallpaper, and the carpet on the stairs was red. The electric lights that lined the wall along the staircase were meant to resemble flickering candles. An antique wooden cabinet stood against the opposite wall. The face of a roaring lion had been carved across its front, and its hand-carved feet were those of an animal with extended claws.

The living room was so full of furniture, there was barely room to move. There were two overstuffed sofas with embroidered covers, and several chairs. There were tables of every shape and size, from low rectangular tables for holding silver tea sets, to short, fat tables for holding piles of magazines, and tall thin tables for holding each of the many lamps with beaded shades. Every table had feet carved like a lion's paws, and so did the piano. A row of yellowed photographs in silver-plated frames lined the mantelpiece.

"It looks like a museum," Carol whispered in awe.

"I think it used to be one."

They looked through four or five rooms before they found one that seemed to belong in the right century. Despite the dark wallpaper and antique furniture, there was a large screen mounted across one wall, and a keyboard next to the bed. A couple of message lights were flashing. Carol keyed in a command to read the messages, and they were projected onto the wall. One was a message from Steve, asking her to get in touch with the office. The other was just a reminder from Face The Music that Sally was overdue for an anti-ageing treatment.

The kitchen was at the rear of the house. Carol sat down while Steve washed the blood from his hands. "What's upstairs?" she asked him.

"Lots of bedrooms. One bathroom. You know even the bathtub's got feet like a lion's paws?"

"You looked in every room?"

"Of course I did."

"Hmm." There was a door next to the oven. Carol got up and opened it. A bare light bulb hung down from the ceiling. She reached up and pulled the cord. The light came on and she headed down the stairs into the basement.

It was a complete contrast to the house upstairs.

The floor was covered with shiny, polished tiles and the walls were panelled and painted white. The furniture was lightweight and modern. There was a music centre with wall-mounted speakers, and a large screen which was currently displaying a typical daytime television programme: an ancient game show from the archives. The sound had been turned down. Carol paused for a moment and watched an hysterical crowd cheer and applaud as a man in a silly hat got a bucket of water thrown over him. Then the camera panned over to a blonde-haired woman in a sequined dress, draping herself across the front of a big black car that ran on gasoline. A fat woman in a trouser suit was escorted onto the stage. The fat woman seemed happy to be there.

Carol felt a hand on her shoulder, and she jumped. "You scared me to death," she scolded Steve. "I didn't hear you."

"Do you smell something?" Steve said.

Carol nodded. He was right; there was a horrible smell in the basement. She noticed a tiny crack of light shining through a door on the far side of the room. She ran over to the door and knocked. "Sally?" She pressed her ear against the door and listened for any sound. She heard nothing. She turned the handle, opened the door, and slammed it shut again.

She rushed past Steve, stumbling up the stairs to the kitchen. She made it to the sink just in time.

Steve followed her, and placed his hands gently on

her shoulders. When she was finished, he helped her over to a chair. She leaned forward, and rested her head on the kitchen table.

"Okay?" Steve said.

Carol closed her eyes and nodded weakly. "You didn't go in there, did you?" she gasped.

"Not yet. I came running after you."

"Thank goodness. Don't you dare go in that room. I don't want you to open that door. Call up the body disposal unit, and tell them specifically that they've got to send *robots*. Understand?"

"Yeah." He went into the bedroom and used the computer. When he came back into the kitchen, he headed straight for the basement door.

"No, Steve!" Carol shouted harshly.

He stopped and looked at her, a puzzled expression on his face.

"I mean it," she said. "Don't go down there."

"I was just gonna turn the TV off."

"Leave it. Let the robots do it. Don't touch anything. With those cuts, you could be extremely vulnerable to infection. In fact, wash your hands again, really thoroughly this time, and then let's go and wait outside."

He shrugged and did as he was told. He'd humoured her before. He could humour her again.

They sat on the front steps and waited for the disposal truck to come. Steve put his arm around her comfortingly, and she rested her head on his shoulder.

When the robots arrived, Carol instructed them to take full precautions with the body. She believed it to be highly infectious, and they were to have themselves and their equipment thoroughly fumigated before they came into contact with any other persons or machinery. The robot who seemed to be in charge assured her that fumigation was standard procedure.

Steve drove Carol home, and promised her that he would take the afternoon off to get a tetanus shot and a complete physical examination. He said he would be back that evening and take her to the hospital to see John. Meanwhile, she was to get some rest.

When Carol got out of the elevator, a little robot was waiting for her. It was just a square box on wheels, with retractable arms and a little red light that began flashing very slowly as it followed Carol back into her apartment. "I don't want anything," she told it. "Just let me sleep a few hours."

It followed her into the bedroom. Grasping the material with its metal claws, it pulled a blanket up over her shoulders.

"Wake me up about six," Carol said, closing her eyes. She fell asleep and dreamed that everyone she'd ever known was still alive.

The little robot stood guard.

Steve did not get a tetanus shot or a physical examination. He drove back to the office.

When Albert saw that Steve was alone, he asked him where Carol was.

"I took her home. Hopefully, she'll get some sleep."

"Some sleep," Albert repeated softly. "Yes, I'm sure that's the best thing."

Steve spent the rest of the afternoon scanning every single one of the company's computers for any signs of malfunction. He ran searches for every known variation of every known computer virus. Nothing showed up in any of the searches, and all the computers now seemed to be working fine. He told himself he knew all along it wasn't a virus.

He left the office a little after seven, and drove over to Carol's apartment. He couldn't stop thinking about the awful smell he'd noticed in Sally's basement. He knew dead bodies started to smell after a while, but the robots said she hadn't been dead long at all – maybe just a few hours.

Just a few hours. If only he'd gone to her house sooner. If only.

He wanted to kick himself.

Amanda opened her eyes and looked at her watch. It was almost eight. I don't believe it, she thought. The alarm didn't go off. She automatically started to phone Hawk Engineering and tell them she'd be late, when she saw that it was dark outside. Then she remembered.

She switched on the light and stood up, staggering a little as she made her way to the kitchen. The box of groceries was still on the floor, exactly where she'd left it. She hadn't even looked inside it. She hoped there was nothing perishable; she'd left it all sitting in a warm room for more than eleven hours. She sat on the floor and went through the box's contents. Most of it was in cans or packets; they would be okay. There was a carton of milk. She opened it and took a sniff. It seemed all right. There was some melted butter and a dozen fresh eggs. She looked up and saw last night's omelette still sitting hardened on a plate. She pulled herself up and carried the plate over to the bin. She lifted the lid and turned the plate upside down. The omelette stayed stuck to the plate. With a sigh, she dropped the whole plate into the bin and replaced the plastic lid.

She reached down to the floor and picked up a packet of artificial bacon. She switched on the oven and draped the slices of bacon across a metal tray. While she was waiting for the bacon to heat up, she made herself a cup of coffee. She put the eggs in the back of the refrigerator, out of sight. They were the last thing she wanted at the moment.

She fluffed up the pillows and then got back into bed, balancing a hot bacon sandwich and a cup of coffee. She reached over to the keyboard and had her messages displayed on the screen.

My dear Amanda,

Thanks for your letter, it was wonderful to hear from you. I'm so pleased you found a job – I knew you could do it. I'm very proud of you – very proud indeed.

I'm afraid I've never heard of a famous entertainer named Olga Jameski, but then as you know, Moscow is a very big place.

Here's an interesting coincidence, though. There is a woman working here at the casino, and you'll never guess what her name is. You've got it in one: Olga Jameski. And she's an American, too. But I'm afraid she isn't an entertainer – she works in the checkroom. So obviously she's not the right Olga, but then Olga is a very popular name here. So don't you worry, honey, I'll keep an eye out for this other Olga Jameski – the famous one – and as soon as I see her I'll be sure to tell her that my niece works with her son. I'm sure she'll be pleased.

Take care of yourself, and write again soon.

 Love,
 Uncle Nathan

Amanda closed her eyes and shook her head. Poor Steve, she thought. His mother's been lying to him.

There was only one hospital. It was usually staffed by about half a dozen doctors, ten nurses, and eight robots. Steve dropped Carol off outside the front door, then drove on to the visitor's parking lot. Carol walked up the steps and pushed her way through a remarkably stiff revolving door. A standard security robot in a grey jumpsuit and white lab coat sat behind a desk in the lobby. "I'm here to visit John McAffrey," she told it.

The robot had a small computer terminal on its desk. It typed in the name, and a short message appeared on the screen. "I'm afraid that patient is not receiving visitors."

"I don't understand."

"I'm afraid that patient is not receiving visitors," the robot repeated, speaking very slowly.

Sometimes they take you so literally, she thought.

Steve came into the lobby. Carol turned to him with an exasperated look.

"Problem?" he said.

"The robot says we can't see John."

"Why not?"

"I haven't got that far yet." She turned back to the robot. "Is there a reason why we can't see him?"

"Yes," replied the robot. "That patient is not receiving visitors."

Steve threw his hands up in mock despair. Carol tried to keep her voice calm as she said to the robot, "Is there someone else we can talk to? Like a doctor?"

"I will see." It typed something and waited. After a moment, it said, "The doctor in charge of the patient is in the building."

"Can we see that doctor?"

The robot turned its attention back to the terminal. Finally, it looked up and pointed to a group of chairs near the front door. "You can wait over there."

It was about twenty minutes before a grey-haired man in a white coat got off the elevator and approached them. "Carol!" he exclaimed as soon as he saw her. She stood up and he rushed over to hug her. "I'm so sorry I kept you waiting. If I'd known it was you, I'd have come running!"

"Hello, Les." She turned to Steve. "This is Steve

Wilson, who works with me, and is really my right-hand man." The doctor grabbed Steve's hand and shook it firmly. Steve winced in pain. His hands were far from healed. "And this is Les Sleski," Carol continued. "The man I owe my life to."

Doctor Sleski took Carol's right hand and gently stroked it, looking down at her partially-missing fingers. "I wish I could tell you that you look wonderful," he said. "But honey, you look absolutely exhausted."

"That's because I am," she said. "A woman named Christine Grinelli died here a couple of days ago."

"Yes, I remember her."

"She was one of my engineers. A woman's body would have been brought here for a post-mortem today. Her name was Sally Hutchins."

"Yes," the doctor said, looking puzzled.

"She worked for me, too. And you've got a patient here, John McAffrey."

"Don't tell me *he's* one of yours, too!"

"That's right. I've known him for thirty years. He used to work with me at the old place, too." She paused to look at the doctor meaningfully. "And the robot says we can't see him."

Doctor Sleski put a finger to his mouth and chewed at the nail, deep in thought.

"And what about Amanda?" Steve said.

The doctor looked up from his fingernail, a question on his face.

"We had a temp at the office all last week," Steve explained, "... and then we had her back again for this week. Yesterday afternoon, she collapsed in the ladies' room. I didn't know about it. I assumed she'd gone home. Then Carol found her late last night. She must've been out for hours."

"You didn't bring her here?" the doctor asked Carol.

"She wouldn't come," Carol shrugged. "She said she felt better. And I didn't know about the others. If I'd had any idea that any of them had died..."

"All right," the doctor said. "But I think I'd better have a look at her. I want her in my office tomorrow. Meanwhile, about John McAffrey... You'd better come upstairs with me."

They took the elevator to the second floor, and followed him down to the end of a long corridor. All the rooms they passed were empty; a lone robot was mopping the floor. They walked through a set of double doors. A sign on the wall read: NO UNAUTHORIZED PERSONS ALLOWED BEYOND THIS POINT. A man sitting behind a desk looked up as they walked in. "It's all right, Sam, they're with me," said the doctor. The man went back to reading his copy of *Really True* magazine.

Doctor Sleski pulled a ring of keys out of his pocket and unlocked a door marked PRIVATE. He switched on the light and closed the door behind them. They were in a small, narrow room about ten feet long and only four feet across. A metal shelf, about one foot deep, ran along the entire length of one wall, at about waist height. A dozen different instruments sat on the shelf, each displaying a reading on a separate bodily function. Beside the instruments, a small microphone sat on a stand. The wall above the shelf was clear glass.

Carol looked through the glass and saw John lying on a bed in the adjoining room, with tubes attached to his arms and up his nose. She turned to the doctor and waited for him to say something. He busied himself checking instruments, and was quiet.

Finally, Steve broke the silence. "What's wrong with him, Doctor?"

"I don't know," Doctor Sleski finally answered. "The robots brought him in last night. The switchboard operator took a call requesting an ambulance at seven o'clock. She said she thought the caller was a child, but when the robots arrived at McAffrey's address, there was no one else with him. Also, according to the robots, McAffrey's apartment was in a real state. Someone had smashed his computer and his wall screen to bits!"

Steve's mouth dropped open in a combination of amazement and disbelief. He looked over at Carol, to see her reaction. She seemed too wrapped up in her own thoughts to even acknowledge his gaze.

"When the dead woman was brought in," Doctor Sleski continued, "and I saw the condition of her body, I had him moved into isolation. We haven't yet identified what killed the two women, but it looks like he's got the same thing. It's obviously a virus, but it isn't one I've encountered before.''

Carol stared through the glass, watching John intently. ''Can I talk to him, Les?''

''He's supposed to be resting.''

''Please, Les, it's important.'' Her lower lip was trembling; she seemed on the verge of tears.

''Okay, use this.'' He sighed as he handed her the microphone. ''You switch it on here. He's wired up so that his voice should come out of that speaker over there. I don't know if he's well enough to answer you, though.''

''Can he see us?'' asked Steve.

''No, it's one-way glass,'' the doctor told him. Steve thought he detected a note of condescension in the doctor's voice. He didn't like it.

''Hello, John. It's Carol. Can you hear me?''

The sound of laboured breathing came over the speaker. ''Where?'' It was barely a whisper. Doctor Sleski turned the speaker volume up.

''John, I'm in the room next to you. Steve's here, too. You know you're in the hospital, don't you?''

The only reply was the sound of his breathing.

''I'll make this quick, John. I don't want to tire you. But listen, this is very important. Can you tell me about how you feel? Tell me your *main symptom*.''

"I can tell you his symptoms," the doctor interrupted.

Carol shushed him and moved closer to the speaker, listening intently. The doctor scowled and crossed his arms, making a little *hmmmph*ing noise.

"I . . ." the voice began weakly. "I can hardly see." There was a pause, then a gulp. "It's like I'm looking out through snow . . . Like I'm surrounded by snow. And . . . and I feel like m-my m-memory's going, Aunty Carol."

"Aunty?" Steve repeated with a puzzled frown.

"Carol, are you all right? You look white as a sheet." Doctor Sleski grabbed hold of her arm and led her firmly towards the door. "Let's get you out of here."

A minute later, she was lying on a sofa in the doctors' lounge, with Les Sleski looming over her, looking concerned. "Maybe I should have you admitted," he said. "You don't look well at all."

"I'm all right, Les. Really."

"You've probably been exposed to whatever McAffrey's got. I'd like to keep you under observation."

"Steve here's been exposed, too. I'm more worried about him. I have reason to believe that I'm immune."

"Now what makes you think that?" the doctor asked in a condescending tone.

"I don't want to tell you just yet, Les. I have a feeling."

"Carol, stop playing games and listen to the doctor," Steve said harshly. "You look terrible."

"You stop playing games and get a tetanus shot," she retorted. "Les, look what he did to his hands today. He cut them on a broken window at Sally Hutchins's house. He swore he'd go to a doctor right away. But as soon as he got rid of me, he went straight to the office!"

"Let's have a look at you," the doctor said to Steve.

"How did you know?" Steve said to Carol, as he reluctantly held out his hands for the doctor. She didn't need to answer. He'd already figured it out for himself. He made a mental note to give Albert a piece of his mind.

"Sam!" Doctor Sleski called from the doorway. "Prepare me a tetanus injection, will you?"

Steve grimaced at Carol and stuck out his tongue.

Doctor Sleski insisted on taking samples of blood from each of them before he would let them leave. Steve had been even less happy about that than getting the injection. There was a scowl on his face as they walked away from the ward.

"Can you meet me out front in about ten minutes?" Carol asked him. "There's something I want to do before I leave."

He sighed and said, "Okay, I'll go get the car." He walked away rubbing his arm.

Carol walked up one flight of stairs. She knew where to go; she had been there before. She walked along the corridor until she came to an arrow pointing to the right. A little hand-written sign above the arrow read MATERNITY. She pushed her way through a pair of swinging doors, and came into another corridor. There was a room on the right behind a large glass wall. Beyond the wall were rows and rows of little cots. She pressed her face against the glass. The room, as usual, was empty. Her breathing formed a mist on the window as she fought to keep back the tears forming at the sight of all those tiny, empty cots.

"Can I help you, Miss?"

Carol turned to face a woman dressed in white trousers and a lab coat. She held a clipboard in one hand, and a stethoscope hung from her neck.

"No." Carol avoided the woman's gaze. "I'm sorry. I was just visiting a friend, and I wanted to see if you had any babies. I was just curious."

"As you can see, there aren't any at the moment. And I'm afraid it's well past visiting hours. I'm going to have to ask you to leave."

"Of course. But can I just ask you, have there been any lately? Any at all?"

"There was one last month. Just in time for Christmas. And loud! You wouldn't believe the lungs on that boy! I don't mind telling you, he really cheered the place up."

"I'll bet he did. Expecting any others?"

"One. In about ten weeks," the woman replied.

"That's good," Carol said softly. "That's very good. That means there's still hope."

"There's always hope," the woman said, handing Carol a handkerchief. She told her she could keep it.

Steve was waiting in the car. "You're a cruel, vicious woman, Carol Hawk," he said as she got in beside him. "You know how I hate needles."

"Shut up and drive. You'd hate lockjaw more."

He shut up and drove. After a while, Carol said, "You can drop me at the office."

"You're not going back there tonight!"

"I want to pick up my car. And I just want to make sure that Albert doesn't let anyone except *me* into the office tomorrow."

"Carol, we discussed this earlier, and I told you I'd take care of everything. I'll phone everyone just as soon as I get home, and I will personally deliver Amanda to your friend the doctor, first thing in the morning."

"You like Amanda, don't you?"

"Know any reason why I shouldn't?" Steve asked her.

"It was just a question. No need to get paranoid."

Steve shook his head and laughed. "Paranoid? Me? That's good coming from you."

Carol deliberately turned away and looked out the window.

"Oh, I meant to tell you," Steve said. "I got your computer working again."

"You shouldn't have been in the office," Carol scolded him. "I told you not to go back there this afternoon. Now this time, I really mean it. *Nobody* goes in that office until I say so. And that definitely includes *you*, Steve."

"Carol, you're over-reacting."

"Am I? What is the only thing that Chris, Sally, John, and now Amanda have in common? The office. I'm closing it down."

"You can't. We've got two projects going."

"I'll just have to go in now and then to check for messages from the field. I can do that on my own."

"But Carol . . ."

"I can't take chances with people's lives, Steve!" The car pulled to a stop in front of the building. "I'll talk to you tomorrow, okay? And thanks for the lift . . . And everything." She slammed the car door and ran into the lobby.

Steve sat in the car for a moment, watching her as she discussed something with Albert. Then he looked down at his bandaged hands and grimaced. That Sam had wrapped him up like a mummy.

He waited until he saw her leave the robot behind in the lobby, and head up the stairs. Then he started the car and drove away. He had work to do.

Carol opened the office door and saw that all the lights were off and everything was quiet. She made her way in the dark to the place where Sally always sat. She sat down in front of Sally's computer and switched it on. The machine clicked and hummed. Carol typed the word **PERSEPHONE**. Orange letters appeared on the screen: **PROGRAM REQUIRED**. She typed in **CHARON**. **USER NAME?** She took a deep breath and typed in **JOHN**. The machine made several clicking noises. There were little flashes of light across the screen. Then the symbol appeared: a little tombstone with **R.I.P.** written across it. She typed in the names of every one of her employees. A tiny coffin appeared on the bottom right-hand corner of the screen. The lid opened with a creak. One by one the names fell into the coffin. When they were all gone, the lid snapped shut and the coffin disappeared.

Suddenly another tombstone appeared, apparently out of nowhere. It was much larger than the previous one; it covered the entire screen. Below the inscription of **R.I.P.**, she saw the words: **WELCOME TO THE SCREEN OF DEATH**. Below that, she saw her own name. She reached down and pulled out the plug.

She sat there in the dark, sweat pouring down her face.

Then she heard something. She stiffened, listening intently. There was a soft hum coming from somewhere near the back of the office. She stood up and walked slowly towards the source of the sound. It was coming from the back room. She opened the door and stepped inside.

The old computer sat buzzing on the table, a faint glow coming from behind its monitor's glass screen. Oh no, she thought. How did *that* get here? She took a deep breath, and carefully moved towards it. A name she hadn't seen or heard in almost twenty years suddenly appeared in large bright letters across the screen.

She screamed and ran out of the room, knocking over the coffee machine on the way. She bruised herself on the edge of a desk, and tripped over a chair. She pulled herself up and kept running until she crashed into something hard and metallic.

"What's the matter, little Muffin?" said the robot.

"Albert! Thank God it's you!"

"Calm down now, little one. Old Grandpop's here. Now what's the problem?"

"Albert, you wouldn't believe what's going on. It's all because of something Mom did a long time ago." She stopped, and threw her hands up in the air. "What am I talking to *you* for?" Her voice became hysterical as the words kept tumbling out. "You're not my great-grandfather! You're not! You're just a stupid robot! You're nothing but a machine. There's nothing *alive* in you, and there never was! You're not like me, and you're not even like *they* were! You're just a hunk of useless metal." The tears she had been fighting all day finally broke loose. She couldn't stop herself; she was sobbing uncontrollably.

The robot put its metal arms around her, letting her tears run down the front of its coat as it lightly stroked her cheek. "There, there," it told her softly.

At nine o'clock the next morning, Amanda answered her phone. "Hey, Amanda. It's Steve here, from Hawk. How are you feeling?"

"I'm a lot better, thank you. I was thinking I'd come in tomorrow..."

"Never mind about that," Steve interrupted. "Can you be dressed and ready to go out in an hour?"

"Huh? Why?"

"I'm sorry, Amanda. I'm not making myself clear. I'm taking you to the doctor today. Doctor's orders, and more importantly, Carol's orders. I'm not supposed to take 'no' for an answer."

"But I don't need to see any doctor."

"He's an old friend of Carol's, so there'll be no

charge, if that's what you're worried about. I'll see you in an hour."

"Oh, Steve! Wait!"

"Yeah?"

Amanda looked up at the letter from her uncle. She'd left it projected on the screen all night. "Uh . . . have you heard from your mother lately?"

"Not lately. Why?"

"Oh, I was just wondering how she was."

"I'm sure she's fine. She's probably just busy. Why do you ask?"

"Just curious."

"Look, I've got to go. I'll talk to you when I see you."

"What happened to your hands?" was the first thing Amanda said when she opened the door.

"Nothing. A little accident," Steve replied with a shrug. "The worst bit was being attacked by a big male nurse."

"Attacked? What do you mean?"

"Yeah, the guy came after me with a hypodermic needle, a roll of gauze, and a gleam in his eye," Steve said dramatically. "I hate hospitals."

"So do I. Let's not go."

"I'm not taking you to the hospital. I'm taking you to an office on Michigan Avenue." He opened his car door with a flourish, and Amanda got inside.

After a few minutes of riding in silence, Amanda

said, "So how long have you been working for Carol?"

"Three years now."

"Three years? So you were only sixteen when you started?"

"About that. You see, Carol knew my mother. And when Mom took off to become a star, Carol promised her she'd look after me. She gave me a job and sort of took me under her wing. I didn't know much of anything when I started," he admitted. "It was Carol that taught me."

"So you were abandoned on Carol's doorstep."

He laughed. "Sort of. But you can't become a star dragging your teenage son around with you, can you? I mean, it can't be easy."

"No, I guess not," Amanda said quietly. "What about your father?"

"Dead a long time ago. I had an older sister, too. She died when I was seven."

"I'm sorry."

He shrugged. "It's no worse than what's happened to you, or anyone else."

"So Carol's like a mother to you, isn't she?"

"I'm not sure about that," he said. "It's true she nags me all the time..."

"Does she?"

"You have no idea!" he said with a mock groan. "But I don't think she's ever tried to replace my mother. We're more like ... friends, I guess. Or even brother and sister, despite the fact she's old enough to be my grandmother."

"Is she? I didn't realize she was *that* old."

"She doesn't look it," Steve admitted. "But then nobody does. They all spend a fortune on treatments to keep them from having a single wrinkle. I tell Carol I think it's stupid – I mean everybody's face looks so plastic. So fake. And then she says you just wait, twenty or thirty years from now you'll change your tune. And then I get mad and say I won't. The way I am now is the way I've always been and the way I'm always going to be. And then she says, you don't know what you're talking about. Everything changes."

He parked the car in front of a high-rise office building. "She makes me mad, sometimes," he said. "But I suppose I love her, really. Platonically, of course." He added something under his breath. Amanda could barely hear him, but it sounded like he said, "Unlike some people I could mention."

Amanda wasn't sure what he meant by that last remark – she wasn't even sure she'd heard him right – so she said nothing. She still said nothing when he put his arm around her in the elevator. She concentrated instead on the building directory mounted next to the row of numbered buttons. SLESKI MEDICAL GROUP was on the fifth floor. There was a cosmetics company on the sixth floor, and something mysteriously labelled PLEASURE, INC., on the seventh. Though the floor numbers went up to twenty, the rest of the directory was blank.

SLESKI MEDICAL GROUP consisted of two smallish rooms. The plaster walls were shot through with hundreds of tiny cracks. Amanda imagined that the walls had once been white.

Steve recognized Sam from the night before. He was sitting behind the reception desk, chewing on a synthetic chicken sandwich and still reading the same issue of *Really True* magazine. There were about four years' worth of back issues piled on top of a folding table in the middle of the room.

Sam nodded at Steve, then turned his gaze to Amanda and told her to go in.

She turned questioningly towards Steve.

"I'll be right here," he told her.

Amanda pushed through a swinging door and found herself face to face with a skeleton, hanging from a coat stand. She turned to her right, and saw a man in a white coat sitting on a folding chair next to an examination table. There was an eye chart on the wall behind him. A large metal cabinet full of glass tubes and strange instruments stood open in the opposite corner.

"I really don't know why I'm here," Amanda began. "I feel all right now. Really."

"I'm glad to hear that," Doctor Sleski replied

brusquely. "But I'd like to have a look at you anyway."

He gestured to the table, and she sat down obediently. He did all the usual things. He listened to her heart, and took her blood pressure. He looked into her eyes, her ears and her throat. He said "Hmmm" and he said "Ahh", and he looked thoughtful. He took some blood and other samples, and then he asked her to describe exactly what had happened two days before.

She told him everything that she remembered. She also told him that she had a history of low blood sugar, and that she had gone without breakfast and lunch on that day, and she didn't remember if she'd eaten dinner the night before. He agreed with her that that may have been the cause. And then he asked her if she noticed anything unusual since she'd been working for Carol.

"Well, there is something. After I'd been there a few days, I started having these dreams."

"What kind of dreams?"

"Oh, silly dreams. Mostly about robots and computers and things."

"Really? I dream about that thing, myself." The doctor pointed to the hanging skeleton. "You can get up now. We're finished."

"How long have you known Carol?" Amanda asked as she was getting dressed.

"Oh, ages! Must be almost twenty years now," he said absently.

"How'd you meet her?"

He was only a young student at the time, in the medical school on the eighth floor of the Audio-techtron building. He'd finished for the day, and was on his way home. He pressed the button to call the elevator and waited. When the doors slid open with a tiny *ping*, he came face to face with a little square box of a robot, carrying an unconscious woman in its arms. There was blood everywhere.

He told Amanda how he'd picked dozens of fragments of glass out of her face and how lucky it was that none of it had gone into her eyes. And he told her how it was the strangest thing, that just before he'd found her in the elevator, all the computer systems in the whole building had malfunctioned, and he hadn't been able to get hold of Doctor Boris, who was his instructor, so it was up to him alone to save her. He still blamed himself for the condition of her right hand. "A trained surgeon could have saved her fingers, but I didn't know what I was doing. I was only a student."

"Why was she in that condition in the first place? What happened to her?" Amanda asked.

"I was never sure of all the details," he replied. "What I understood at the time was that some equipment in the basement had blown up. Carol still worked for Audiotechtron in those days, you see."

"Audiotechtron?" Amanda said, remembering the computer printouts back at the office. "What kind of company was Audiotechtron? What did they do?"

The doctor looked amazed. "What did Audiotechtron do? They did everything. You know the robots you see every day?"

Amanda nodded.

"They were all built by Audiotechtron. And that was only one small part of their business. Their biggest success – and also their biggest failure – was the development of artificial intelligence. That's what closed them down in the end. But I guess you were just a baby when that happened."

"And Carol used to work for them?"

"Oh, yes," Doctor Sleski said. "She was one of their big wheels. The biggest." He went on to tell her how after Carol had regained consciousness, the company chairman had spent hours and hours talking to her. And he'd heard that when they'd opened the door to Carol's office, everything in the room had been completely buried in paper. They said at the time that every file in the entire network had been printed out, and those printed files would serve as a kind of reference library when the time came to build a new computer network to replace the one that had just been dismantled.

"But of course, it wasn't all the network's files, after all," the doctor added sadly. "The system crashed long before the printing was anywhere near finished.

Much later, I heard a rumour that ninety percent of the printout was pre-war accounting records."

Amanda gasped, again remembering the printouts.

"Pretty useless stuff, really," the doctor went on. "They also said there were some formulas for age-delaying skin creams, and a few designs for outdated equipment. But that was all. Even the medical research files had been lost, and none of us in the medical school had completed our training! We all just gathered together, copied each other's course notes and went into practice. We had to. There were no doctors anywhere, once the computer network crashed."

"But you mentioned something about your instructor. You said he was called Doctor Boris?"

Doctor Sleski shook his head. "Doctor Boris was an AI. AI's did everything in those first years after the war. Without them, we would have been lost."

"If you would have been lost without them, then how come they were banned?"

The doctor's expression turned cold. He turned away and started to write out a prescription. "I don't have all day to sit here chatting, you know. Take one of these twice a day and you'll be fine."

Steve put down his back issue of *Really True* and stood up when Amanda came into the waiting room. "Everything all right?"

"He gave me a prescription for iron supplements; other than that he says I'll live."

"Good," said Steve. "So what do you think of him?"

"The doctor?" Amanda said. "To tell you the truth, I think he's a little weird."

"I'm glad to hear it. I don't like him, either." He took her arm and led her out of the office. "Do you have any plans for this evening?"

"Not really. Why?"

"Well, I was wondering if you might like to come out for a drink later. If you feel well enough, that is."

"I feel well enough."

"Great. I've got some things I've got to do this afternoon. Things for work. You know. But I can pick you up about . . . eight?"

"Eight's fine."

Steve went back to his apartment, made himself a sandwich, and sat down in front of his home computer. He typed in a few commands, and projected the files he was reviewing onto his big wall-mounted screen. He leaned back in his chair, and stared at the magnified words and diagrams covering an entire wall of his apartment. The more he studied the files he'd copied from the old computer, the more he became convinced that he had rediscovered the original designs for the prototype voice-responsive computer with artificial intelligence. He took a bite of his sandwich, and typed in another file name: **SAMSON**.

Hours later, Steve was still staring at the screen, trying to make sense of what he was reading. He could understand the mechanical references all right. Wiring, chips and circuit boards posed no problem. But he couldn't figure out what words like "gamete" and "zygote" were doing in there.

Sometimes he found it easier to think if he was moving around. He got up and started to walk around the room, clicking his fingers in rhythm with his steps. The bandages on his hands were bothering him. He stopped to pull them off, and happened to glance at his watch. It was seven forty-five. "Oh no!" he exclaimed, racing into the bathroom.

It was nearly eight-thirty when Amanda heard the buzz of her doorbell. "Sorry I'm late," Steve said into the intercom.

"No problem. I'll be right down."

She went downstairs and opened the front door to see Steve dressed in a dark blue suit and a bright red tie. His hair was still wet from the shower, and he was carrying a bunch of flowers. He thrust the flowers at her. "These are for you."

"Wow!" Amanda said. "What are they, roses?"

He nodded.

"Wherever did you get them?"

"I'll show you sometime," he said, deliberately sounding mysterious.

"I guess I should put these in water. That's what

you're supposed to do with flowers, isn't it? Uh … come in!''

He followed her into her apartment, and headed straight for her computer. ''Erebus Series Five. Not a bad little machine! I didn't think they still made them.''

''They probably don't. It belonged to my aunt, and she got it second-hand. They told her the previous owner was a little old lady who only used it on Sundays – that was some kind of joke, apparently. It doesn't have a lot of functions, but it's good enough for me, anyway. The fancy ones always break down. Or at least they do when I try to use them.'' She looked through all her kitchen cupboards. ''I'm afraid I don't have a vase,'' she said apologetically. ''I'll have to put them in a glass. What a shame I can't do them justice.''

''I think you do,'' Steve said.

Amanda's cheeks felt like they were on fire. She turned away quickly and busied herself with the roses.

''That's a nice dress.''

''Thanks,'' she said, not turning away from the roses.

''Nice place,'' he said.

''It was my aunt's. Everything you see was my aunt's.'' She walked over to the door. She felt so nervous she could hardly keep from shaking. She couldn't understand why she felt that way; she'd been perfectly comfortable with Steve at the office. But that was work, and that was daylight. This was night, and it was different. "Shall we go?" she said, looking straight ahead.

"Is there a particular place you'd like to go?" Steve asked her on the way downstairs.

She shrugged. "I'm open to suggestions."

"Ever been to the Penthouse?"

"Steve, the truth is I've hardly been anywhere."

"You'll like the Penthouse," he said as they got in the car.

He turned west on Randolph, and drove past several blocks of vacant lots and boarded-up buildings before he pulled up in front of a small, squat, one-storey building of crumbling brick. The door looked like nothing more than a sheet of corrugated iron. Amanda couldn't see any windows.

She got out of the car and looked up and down the street. It was pitch dark. The whole neighbourhood would have seemed deserted, if it wasn't for the fact that there were about a dozen cars plugged into the side of the building.

Steve pulled back the iron door, and she hesitantly followed him inside. As they walked down the dimly lit hall, Amanda found herself getting nervous all over again, and for a different reason this time. She couldn't stop herself wondering exactly what Steve was up to. They were all by themselves in what seemed like an abandoned warehouse in the middle of nowhere. What kind of place was this to take someone on a date? And how well did she know this guy, anyway? Not well at all. She'd only just met him, really.

She tried to console herself with the fact that she'd never known of a single violent crime in her lifetime. That was one of the few advantages of a greatly reduced population: psychotic murderers and robbers were all part of the past, she reminded herself. You only read about them in history books.

They stopped in front of an elevator. Steve smiled at her, and she tried to smile back. Stop being so paranoid, she scolded herself.

Steve pressed the call-button, and the elevator door slid open. They stepped into a brightly-lit, wood-panelled interior. A large round mirror, framed in gold leaf, hung on one wall. Amanda watched from the corner of one eye as Steve glanced in the mirror and smoothed down his hair. The door slid silently closed behind them.

They stood facing another door, with two rows of numbered buttons mounted on the wall beside it. Above the door, a digital display read: GROUND FLOOR. Next to the button numbered thirty-eight, there was a little gold-coloured metal plaque, ornately engraved with the words PENTHOUSE BAR. Steve pressed the button for thirty-eight. The elevator shook and bumped while the digital display above the door went through all the numbers between two and thirty-seven. Finally, the display read PENT-HOUSE. The door slid open and Amanda gasped in amazement.

They stepped out into what appeared to be a large circular room high above the city. The room had been decorated in an understated turn-of-the-century style: smoky-grey mirrors and thick grey carpet. The antique cocktail tables were sparkling chrome, and the chairs were upholstered in padded imitation black leather. The bar itself was a combination of chrome and black leather. There was a raised stage area with a piano and a microphone. But the out-standing feature was the view.

The entire room was surrounded by a floor to ceiling window. Straight ahead, Amanda could see down to Lake Shore Drive, where the headlights of dozens of cars zoomed by in both directions. Beyond them the waters of Lake Michigan glistened blackly beneath the stars. On the opposite side of the room, a seemingly endless horizon of high-rise buildings stretched into the distance for miles and miles, a light shining brightly in every window.

They sat at a table overlooking the lake. "It's beautiful," Amanda said. "Completely convincing." So different from the reality of deserted streets, uninhabited buildings in various states of decay, and vast areas of empty, dead space where nothing grew.

"What would you like?" asked Steve.

The bartender picked up a bottle labelled *Scotch*

Flavoured Alcohol, and poured some brown liquid into two glasses. Steve brought them back to the table just as a robot dressed in a black suit and a big bow tie was making its way to the stage.

The robot bowed, and said, "Evenin' all," into the microphone. Then it picked up a glass, stuck a one dollar bill inside it, and put it on top of the piano. With no further ado, the robot sat down and began to play.

"Do you like this place, Amanda?"

"I love it. It's brilliant."

"I'm really glad you do," Steve said shyly. "I was the one who designed it."

"What do you mean? Do you own the place or something?"

"Oh no, nothing like that. It was just a bit of moonlighting I did, about a year ago. When I say I designed it, I don't mean that I chose the furniture or anything. But I did all the animation for the windows, built the elevator, programmed the robots . . . stuff like that."

"How did you program a robot to play the piano?"

"Well, I didn't really. The piano plays itself."

"I'm still impressed. When did you find the time to do it?"

He shrugged. "Evenings, weekends." He took off his glasses and rubbed his eyes. "What else was there to do? It was just a way of filling the time."

He's not bad looking, Amanda found herself

thinking. He's got a nice face. "You spend all your time working, don't you?"

"That's something I'd like to change. You have no idea how much."

Amanda looked down at her drink. She'd never drunk alcohol before, and it was obvious she didn't have much of a tolerance for it. She'd only had one Scotch, and she could already feel her face getting warm. She hoped her cheeks weren't turning red again.

"Would you like another one?" Steve asked her.

"Not right now. In a minute."

"When you do, just say the word." He reached forward and touched her on the arm, a mischievous expression on his face. "Look behind you," he told her. "I spent *months* on her."

Amanda looked up to see another robot approaching the stage. But this one was different. A sequined gown clung tightly to its metal body. Its long brown wig was parted on the side, so that some hair could be draped provocatively over one camera lens eye. Its stainless steel hands had been finished with long red fingernails.

The robot positioned itself in front of the microphone, and a woman's voice came from its motionless speaker of a mouth. "Hi, everybody. Welcome to the Penthouse. I hope you're all having a wonderful time, 'cause I sure know that I am. My name's Samantha, and I'd like you to meet my old buddy,

Max Rogers, on keyboards!" Samantha led the applause for the piano-playing robot. It ran one hand along the keys with a flourish and waved at the audience.

"And now," Samantha continued, "I'd like to sing you an old, old song. It's one of my favourites, and I hope it's one of *your* favourites, too." Max Rogers played the intro, and Samantha launched into a slow and soulful rendition of *Stormy Weather*.

It was nearly three when Steve pulled up in front of Amanda's place. She made no move to get out of the car. Her head was thrown back against the seat cushion and her eyes were closed. Her breathing was deep and rhythmic. Steve leaned over to her and said, "Wake up. You're home."

"Hmm?" She opened her eyes. "Oh, yeah."

"I'll walk you to the door."

"You're a perfect gentleman."

He gave her one of his smiles, and said, "Don't count on it."

Amanda was a little unsteady on her feet. She'd only had two drinks before she'd switched to fizzy orange, but she felt warm and tingly all over, and just a little light-headed. She stopped in front of the door and said, "Thank you, Steve. I've had a really nice evening."

He leaned forward and kissed her, but she pushed him away after only a few seconds.

"Is something the matter?" he said.

"Nothing."

"In that case . . ." he said, moving his face close to hers.

"Steve, I'm really tired. I've had a wonderful night, but I've also had a really long day, and you know I've been ill . . ."

"I forgot all about that!" he interrupted. "I'm a thoughtless jerk, you know that? Maybe tomorrow, huh?"

"What about tomorrow?" She felt a little hazy.

"I want to see you."

"Well . . . Steve, I . . ."

He took one of her hands and pressed it against his cheek. Then he gave her one of his calculated little-boy-lost looks.

"Okay," she said. "Call me."

Steve opened the door to his apartment and saw that he'd left his wall screen on. The same incomprehensible words and equations were still on display. He checked his console. There were no message lights flashing. Strange, he thought. I should have heard from Carol by now. He looked at the time: nearly three-thirty, too late to call her now. He made a mental note to call her first thing when he got up, switched off the screen, and went to bed.

He woke up at ten o'clock, did a shortened version of his usual morning karate workout, and phoned Carol's apartment. No answer.

He phoned the office. No answer. He phoned Doctor Sleski. John had died, and now Julio was sick. The doctor hadn't heard from Carol. Steve phoned

Albert. The robot told him how worried he was. He'd never seen her so upset, and the office was a mess.

"What do you mean about the office being a mess?" Steve asked him.

"Broken things everywhere," Albert lamented.

"What's broken?"

"Chairs, machines, everything."

"And what about Carol? Is she with you now?"

"She said she was going home," Albert moaned.

"She's not there. I've been trying to phone her."

"That's what she told me," said the robot. "She said she was going home."

Steve tried her apartment again. Still no answer. He typed a brief message on his keyboard, and transmitted it to her home computer.

Then he got into his car and drove to the office.

Albert stood up when he saw him. "Sorry, Steve. I can't let you go up there."

"Don't be ridiculous, Albert."

"That's what Carol told me. No one is to be allowed into the office. And then she said, 'Tell Steve that means *him.*'"

"Look, Albert. No one has seen or heard from Carol since Wednesday night. Aren't you worried about her?"

"You know I'm worried sick, Steve. I'm worried sick."

"If we're going to find her, I've gotta have a look at the office. You understand that, don't you?"

"I guess I understand, Steve. I'm worried sick."

He patted the robot on the back, and raced up the stairs. The office door was open. Albert was right. The place was a mess. Several desks, including his, had been knocked over. His computer was lying face down on the floor. The wires had been cut and the circuit boards ripped out. All the other terminals were in the same condition. Further back, the coffee machine was lying face down, too. The carpet around it was soaked. Damp lumps of powdered milk had hardened on the floor. He stepped over the coffee machine and the puddle around it, and carefully made his way into the back room.

The old computer was sitting on the table where he'd left it, but with its cover pulled off and its guts torn out. A broken chair lay on the floor in front of it. The monitor's glass screen was cracked.

He heard footsteps. He looked up, and saw the robot standing behind him. "Albert, I don't understand. Who did this?"

"Carol," the robot replied.

"CAROL? Why?"

The robot was silent for a moment. "Carol said that Christine and Sally were both dead. Is that true, Steve?"

"I'm afraid so."

Albert lowered his head. "That means I'll never see them again, doesn't it?"

"Yes, Albert. That's right."

"Carol said John was going to die, too." The robot folded its metal hands and raised them to its motionless mouth. "That means I won't see him again, either."

"John did die," Steve said softly.

"That's what comes of being old," the robot muttered. "Your friends all leave you, one by one, until you're the only one left." It raised its head and looked directly at Steve. "Carol was really upset, Steve. I never saw her so unhappy. And then she took a deep breath and she pulled herself up straight and she became very calm. She told me you were all going to die unless she did something about it."

"Did she tell you what she was going to do?" Steve asked the robot anxiously.

"This is what she did Steve," the robot said, indicating the state of the room. "She was very methodical. She cut all the phone lines, too."

"Why didn't you stop her?"

"She told me not to," said the robot matter-of-factly. "And then she told me she was going home to 'finish the job'. That's what she said."

"It doesn't make sense," Steve said more to himself than to Albert. "After all the work she's put into this company."

"Steve?"

"Yeah, Albert."

"I will see Muffin again, won't I?"

Carol's apartment was on the fifteenth floor of a building in the old downtown business district, near the river.

Steve parked his car right outside the building's revolving door. Just inside the entrance, a little set of five steps led up to a glass door that was always kept locked. There was a small video camera above the door, and the building directory was mounted on the wall next to an intercom.

Though there were nearly a hundred apartments in the building, there were only fourteen names in the directory. Each name had its own four-digit code number. The number next to "Hawk, C." was 2501. Steve keyed in the number and waited as her intercom rang. He didn't really expect Carol to answer, so he was surprised when he heard a little *click* come from the speaker.

"Carol?" he said into the mouthpiece. No answer. "Carol!" he said again, louder. Nothing. Then he remembered Carol's little robot: the box on wheels. As far as Steve was concerned, the stupid thing was totally useless and should have been scrapped years ago. It was one of those many incomprehensible quirks in Carol's character, that not only wouldn't she get rid of it, she wouldn't even consider adjusting its program.

"Alphonse, is that you?" he said gently, as if he were speaking to a little child. "Alphonse, it's Steve. Carol's friend. You've seen me lots of times. If you press the red button by the door, you can see my face."

He looked up at the camera and waved. "See, it's *me*, Alphonse. You know me, don't you? Now if you press the *blue* button, I can come inside." He waited. Nothing happened. He looked back up at the camera and smiled. He heard another little *click* from the speaker.

The robot had hung up.

Steve turned back to the intercom and keyed in the code number again. It rang a couple of times, and then there was a little *click*.

"Alphonse, you little monster," Steve said slowly and menacingly. "If you don't let me in, I'm going to kick in this door, and then I'm going to come upstairs, fill up the bathtub, drop you in and leave you to rust. If you don't want me to do that, you'd better press that blue button and let me inside. Right now."

There was a moment's silence. "Okay, Alphonse, it's the bathtub for you," Steve said threateningly. There was a click and a buzz; then the downstairs door flew open.

Steve had always hated the lobby of Carol's building. The foyer walls were covered with a hideous shiny silver wallpaper that had a pattern of raised blue velveteen flowers. The furnishings consisted of two sofas upholstered in a cheap polyester material that also had a raised blue velveteen floral print and one chrome and glass coffee table. There was the obligatory screen mounted high on the wall directly opposite the sofas. The screen was currently showing another classic game show from the archives: something called *Pyramid of Money*. Steve glanced up on his way to the elevator, and saw the smiling face of a woman who'd died long before he was born.

He pressed the call button and waited for the lift. He tried to remember the last time he'd felt afraid, and then he came to the conclusion that he had never really felt fear until now. He hadn't been the least bit afraid the other day, when they'd broken into Sally's house. But then, he'd never expected to find her dead. He didn't want to think about what he might find today.

The ride to the fifteenth floor seemed to take an eternity. He looked down at his hands. They were shaking.

Finally, the elevator doors slid open and he stepped out onto Carol's floor. The little robot was standing in the hall, waiting for him. The door to Carol's apartment was open.

Steve walked past the robot and into the apartment. He felt his throat tighten as he called Carol's name. "Carol!" he shouted hoarsely. "Carol!"

Her apartment consisted of one long hallway lined

on both sides with doors leading off to different rooms. Steve methodically opened every door and looked inside. There was no sign of her.

He turned around to face the little robot, who had been following him the whole time. "Look, Alphonse," he said to the metal box, "has she been here?"

The robot just stood where it was.

"I know you can't talk, but you can *understand*, right?"

The robot didn't move.

"What I want you to do is lift your right arm if she's been here in the last two days, and lift your left arm if she hasn't. So it's right arm for yes, and left arm for no."

The robot did nothing.

"Right for yes, left for no," Steve said again. "Alphonse, has Carol been here at all in the last two days?"

The robot made a little clicking noise. Then it lifted up both of its arms.

"Okay," Steve said. He went into the bathroom and switched on the taps.

The robot rolled into one of the bedrooms and slammed the door shut. Steve could hear it piling furniture against the door.

He went back into the living room, where Carol kept her little home computer hooked up to an antique nineteen-inch black and white television set.

He'd never understood why such a technically proficient person should have the most primitive home computer imaginable. He moved her sewing basket to one side, and sat down to read her messages.

Hello, Carol. Couldn't get through to the office! Anyway, just to let you know that final station inspection is due for Friday, so if all goes well, I'll be back in the office first thing Monday. Feel free to contact me if any queries. Kath.

That was from Katherine, chief engineer on the California project. They were finishing up right on schedule.

Nobody answering phones, and office system appears to be down. Problems on site. Please contact Jaime Gonzales in Lima, pronto. Jim.

Steve just shrugged when he saw that one. It wasn't the first time they'd had problems in Peru.

Carol, I've been trying to phone you, both at home and at work. Urgent that I talk to you. Les.

Steve didn't like that word "urgent". Of course, it might just be that he wanted to tell her about Julio. He hoped that was all it was.

CAROL! WHAT THE BLAZES IS GOING ON? WHY IS NO ONE ANSWERING THE PHONE, AND WHAT HAS HAPPENED TO THE SYSTEM? I'VE BEEN

TRYING TO CONTACT YOU ALL HOURS OF THE DAY AND NIGHT, BUT NO REPLY. PROTECTIVE CLOTHING HAS NOT BEEN DELIVERED, NOW I AM TOLD IT WAS NEVER ORDERED. WORK IS AT A STANDSTILL. CLIENT IS UNHAPPY. ENGINEERS ARE UNHAPPY. I AM UNHAPPY, DO SOMETHING! JIM.

Steve decided that Jim had better be told what was going on. He was just about to pick up the phone, when it started ringing.

"Hello?" Steve said.

"Is Carol there?" a man's voice asked.

"No, she isn't. Who's calling?"

"Please just ask her to phone Les Sleski."

"Doctor Sleski? It's Steve Wilson here."

"Oh, Steve! Have you heard from her yet?"

"No, Doctor. That's why I'm here. I was looking for her."

"I see," the doctor said dejectedly.

"Doctor, I've seen the message you left for Carol. Why did you say it was 'urgent' to speak to her? It's not to do with those blood samples you took, is it?"

"Well, actually it is," the doctor began.

Steve gasped, a sharp intake of breath so loud he was certain the doctor could hear it. Calm down, he scolded himself. You've got to keep in control.

"Of course, I should probably tell you off for reading other people's messages," the doctor continued, "but this time it's nothing to worry about."

120

Steve forgot all about staying calm and in control. "NOTHING TO WORRY ABOUT?" His voice was bordering on hysteria. "Three people I work with are dead, one's in hospital, my boss has disappeared, and you're telling me there's nothing to worry about?"

"Calm down, Steve," the doctor said quietly. "We have finally managed to isolate the virus, and I can tell you that we didn't detect it in your blood sample. So for the moment at least, you're all right, though we did find some interesting antibodies that we're still having a look at. Does that make you feel any better?"

Steve hated the patronizing tone the doctor was using with him, but he managed to keep his temper in check. "And what about Amanda?" he asked huskily.

"You want to know everything, don't you? Oh, all right. There's nothing wrong with her. Slightly anaemic, that's all. I've already put her on supplements."

"And Carol?"

"Now that's a slightly different matter, Steve. I don't think I should discuss it with you."

"You'll discuss it with me now, over the phone," Steve said, struggling to keep his voice even, "or you'll discuss it with me in person, while I repeatedly bash your stupid head into a wall!"

"There's no need to take that tone with me, Steve. Surely you must accept the principle of confidentiality between . . ."

"I don't care about your principles! Carol and I go back a long way, and for all I know, she's lying somewhere . . . dying. I don't know where to look for her, I don't know what to do!" He clenched his fists in frustration; his eyes were starting to water. Stop that, he told himself, angrily wiping a tear from his cheek.

"Steve, Steve," the doctor said soothingly. "Of course you're worried about her. I understand that. Look, I'm sure that wherever Carol is, she's probably all right."

"Why?" Steve croaked. "How do you know?"

"Okay, I suppose I can tell you. We *did* find the virus in Carol's blood . . ."

"Oh, God!"

"But the virus was dead. Do you understand me? *The virus was dead.*"

"Wh–what?" Steve stammered.

"Do you remember the other night at the hospital, when Carol said she thought she was immune?" There was a pause. "Well, it looks like she is. That's why I've got to talk to her. How did she know she was immune? Imagine how important that is, if we're going to develop a vaccine."

Steve had always been clever. He'd been a bright little boy and then the whizz-kid of the office. Carol's special protégé, the one she always said would take over when she retired. And now he was stuck in the middle of something he just couldn't understand. He felt slow and stupid; he couldn't think. "If I see Carol, I'll tell her," was all he said.

He hung up the phone and sat down. Jim's latest message was still projected on the wall: **CAROL! WHAT THE BLAZES IS GOING ON?** He wouldn't phone Jim just yet. He didn't know what to tell him.

He took a piece of paper and a pen from a drawer and wrote: "Carol, I was here looking for you. Doctor Sleski wants to talk to you urgently, also you have important messages on the computer." He'd forgotten about the message he'd sent from his own computer that morning, otherwise he might have wondered why it wasn't there. "Please contact me. If I'm not at home, then..." he thought for a moment before he added, "try Amanda's." He placed the note across her keyboard. It was the one place she'd be certain to find it ... if she ever came back.

There was a spare set of keys hanging on a hook in the kitchen. Steve put them in his pocket before he left.

11

Steve climbed the three flights of stairs to his apartment. Like Amanda, he was the only person living in his building. He'd chosen the top floor because it had a skylight. The bedroom was a cluttered mess, with a workbench, tools, and various bits and pieces of machinery and wiring scattered across every available surface. But he'd managed to keep the living room as an almost empty space – dominated by its huge wall screen. He kept the furniture and console well away from the section of floor he used for karate practise. He'd already reached brown belt level through a video correspondence course. He kept meaning to send for the black belt disk, but just hadn't found the time.

On the drive home, Steve had worked out his plan

of action. First, he was going to call the police and report Carol as a missing person. Second, he was going to phone Jim and tell him what had happened. And finally, he was going to call Amanda and explain why he probably wouldn't see her again tonight, after all.

When Steve opened his door, the first thing he noticed was that the wall screen was on, still displaying that same incomprehensible file. That was strange. He was certain he'd switched it off. But then he told himself it wasn't impossible that he'd forgotten; the events of the last few days had definitely rattled him.

He switched the screen off, and took the phone into the bedroom. He tried to call the police switchboard. Nothing happened. It wasn't even ringing. He dialled the number again. Still nothing.

He tried to phone Jim, in Peru. The same thing happened. He muttered an obscenity. His phone was dead.

He pulled off the plastic cover and looked inside. Everything seemed okay.

He went back into the living room, and typed a message for the police into the computer. He entered a code number and pressed the key for transmission. Next, he typed a letter to Jim, telling him what had happened, and that he had reported Carol as a missing person. He took a deep breath before he pressed the transmission key on that one. Then he typed a short note to Amanda, saying he was sorry he was going to have to break their date, but he would explain everything when he saw her. He was about to type in her transmission code, when these words appeared across the little screen on his console: **WHO IS AMANDA?**

"HUH?" Steve said out loud. He pushed his chair back and frowned at the screen. It went dark for a moment, and then letter by letter, these words were formed: **AMANDA IS A USER NAME RECOGNIZED BY CHARON. THE NAME WAS NOT RECOGNIZED BY THE SYSTEM UNTIL 1400 HOURS ON THE TWENTY-FIRST DAY OF JANUARY. IT IS A NEW USER NAME, AND NOT ON THE LIST OF HAWK EMPLOY-EES. REPEAT: WHO IS AMANDA?**

Steve thought for a moment, and then he leaned forward and typed: **SO WHO WANTS TO KNOW?**

THE SCREEN OF DEATH DECREES THIS SCREEN MUST DIE. HA HA.

A tiny tombstone appeared, then vanished. There was a popping sound, and the little screen on Steve's console went blank. Steve stood up and walked around behind the console, clicking his fingers in thought. He went into the bedroom and got his toolbox. He took out a tiny screwdriver, and started removing all the little screws that held the console together. He was just about to remove the cover, when he heard a loud crackling noise and saw a flash of light. He swung around and saw that his wall screen had come back on. A switch on the console board flipped over all by itself. It stopped at the setting labelled "television".

"And now, for your viewing pleasure," said the mellow voice of a professional announcer, "we bring you another classic from the Golden Age of Television: *What's My Living?*" There was an opening shot of the studio audience applauding, and then the entire screen became filled with the face of a little boy.

"Hello, Steve," the little boy said cheerfully.

"Who are you?" What am I doing, talking to him, Steve thought. It's not like he can hear me!

"I'm your little brother."

"I don't have a little brother," Steve said firmly. He *can* hear me, he thought.

"Sure you do! Didn't Aunty Carol ever tell you about me?"

"Carol's your aunt, and I'm your brother? I don't think that's possible."

"Well, Carol isn't really my *aunty*," the little boy said, coyly leaning his head to one side. "I just call her that. She's more like my cousin, really. But you're definitely my brother. We've got the same parents!"

Steve stood with his arms crossed in front of him. "Oh, do we? Just for the record, what were their names?"

"Oh, that's easy. Our mother's name was Annette Stevens, and our father was Joe Wilson," the boy answered. "They only got married two weeks before you were born," he added confidentially.

Steve hadn't heard about that before. "Who put you up to this?" he demanded.

The little boy ignored the question, and carried on talking. "And we had a sister named Jenny, but she didn't live long, did she? And then there's me, and there were four others, too. Two boys and two girls. Didn't Aunty Carol tell you about them either?"

"Two boys and two girls," Steve repeated ironically. "Oh, really. So what were their names?"

"One oh one, one oh two, one oh three, and one oh four," the boy replied.

Oh boy, Steve thought. A real nutcase! Or somebody's sick idea of a joke.

"And do you know what happened to them? Aunty Carol murdered them!" The boy's face twisted with rage. "She killed them in cold blood! I saw her. She ripped them apart! Our little brothers and sisters."

"Carol ripped them apart, did she?"

"Yes, and she killed the others, too."

"The others?"

"She even killed Samson," the little boy sniffed.

Samson? Steve tried to remember where he'd seen that name. Then he realized that it was the name of the file he'd had projected on his screen until just a few minutes ago. The kid must have got the name from his file directory.

"Can I ask you something, kid?"

"Yeah, sure," the boy replied brightly.

"How come you can hear me? I don't have that kind of a set-up."

"I modified your system."

"Yeah? Well modify *this*," Steve said as he pulled out the plug. The screen went blank.

Steve had built his entire home computer system himself from scratch. It was his baby; his pride and joy. The fact that anyone would dare to tamper with it made him furious. He went into the bedroom and put on his coat. With his phone dead, and his computer disconnected, the only way to get to the police was in person. He could drive to the station in less than fifteen minutes. He was going to make sure that whoever had done this was going to end up either in jail or in the hospital. Or both.

He picked up his car keys and headed for the door. It wouldn't open. "Why'd you do that, Steve?" asked the voice of a child. Steve turned around and faced the screen. The little boy was back on the wall. He smiled, and pushed some hair back from his face.

"WHO ARE YOU?"

"I told you. I'm your little brother. My name is Tom."

Steve kept struggling with the door. Finally, he quit in exasperation. "Okay, how do you do it?"

"Do what?"

"I unplugged everything!"

"That doesn't matter. I don't need cables or anything. That's the way Aunty Carol designed me."

"You said Carol 'designed' you? That's what you said?"

"That's right."

"I thought you said you were my brother."

"That's right, too. That's why you're going to help me, aren't you? I was sick for a really long time, but I'm better now. I was in a coma, unconscious, and they all thought I was dead. But I didn't die; I was too strong to die. And you know what? I'm getting stronger and stronger all the time now." Tom beamed at Steve with a broad smile that revealed the gap between his two front teeth.

"Glad to hear you're better, kid. Of course, I'll be glad to help you," Steve said in a deliberately casual tone. "What do you want me to do?" He looked up at the face on the screen and decided to try a small test. He waved his arms around and made a couple of faces. The boy didn't react at all. He could hear, but he couldn't see.

Meanwhile, Tom hadn't stopped talking. He told Steve that Carol must be punished, along with all her accomplices. Then Tom went on to tell Steve that he could be a great help to his little brother if he'd just key in the transmission codes for every person who worked for Carol. Then as soon as she got in touch with any of them, it would be easy to trace her.

"So what you want to do is to connect up to everybody's home computers, is that it?" Steve asked.

"Sure," Tom answered with a smile. "Just like I'm connected up to yours. That way, I can keep an eye on everybody at once. We'll be like one big happy network!"

130

"Not big," Steve corrected him. "There's only me and a couple of others. And she probably won't get in touch with any of us anyway, if she hasn't so far."

"I guess you've got a point there, big brother," Tom said with a shrug of his shoulder. "I know it wouldn't be the first time she left someone to die."

"Uh-huh," Steve said, pursing his lips in thought. "And what happens if I don't give you these codes?"

"I can get them anyway. Like you said, there's only a couple. I'll control every terminal in the world soon, anyway. You saw some of what I can do, the other day at Hawk."

"I don't know what you're talking about. What did I see?"

"I made the letters fall down," the little boy giggled. "That was fun."

"So that was you! I knew it wasn't a virus."

The little boy's face hardened. "You think you know a lot. But you don't know anything. Not anything at all. So don't get any silly ideas that I need you, 'cause I don't. I've already been through all your files, and all the files at Hawk. The only thing I haven't found is those transmission codes, but I can just key in numbers at random until I finally get them – that won't take me any time at all. I only thought I'd keep you alive for a while, on account of you're my brother. I thought it might be interesting if we got to know each other first."

"I see," Steve said. "Look, I can save you a bit of

trouble, if you'll just give me a minute. I've got all those codes you need, but they're in the other room, so you'll have to excuse me for a minute while I go and get them. Then I'll hook you up to anybody you want. It'll be fun; we'll have a party." Remembering that Tom couldn't see, he reached for the window. It wouldn't open. He was about to kick through the glass, when the thought of what he'd done to his hands the other day stopped him. He went into the bedroom and put on two pairs of gloves.

"I want *all* the codes you've got, Steve," Tom called from the living room. "There's really more than just a couple. You've got people out in the field, too, haven't you? And don't forget that new name: Amanda. I want to talk to Amanda; I want to show her my Screen of Death. That'll be fun, huh?"

"I won't forget Amanda!" Steve yelled back. He came out of the bedroom and walked straight over to the window. He hesitated for a moment as he looked through the glass. After all, it was three floors down to the street.

"What are you doing, Steve?"

"Nothing." Steve swung around and shattered the glass with the heel of his boot.

"Steve! Steve! Where are you?" Tom sounded like he was about to cry.

Steve climbed out the window and jumped to the ground.

Amanda was dreaming again. She was dreaming that she was the guest of honour at a banquet. She was sitting alone at a long table on top of a platform. A uniformed waiter kept bringing her more and more platters piled with food. She kept trying to tell him that she just couldn't eat any more, but something was wrong with her voice. It seemed like every time she opened her mouth to speak, all that came out was: "BUZZ!" She looked up to see a swarm of bees flying towards her. The buzzing got louder and louder...

BUZZZZZZ!

"All right, all right. I'm coming." She sat on the edge of the bed, holding her head in her hands.

BUZZZZZZZZZ!

"All right! I've said I'm coming!" She stumbled over to the door. "Whaddya want?" she mumbled into the intercom.

"Amanda, let me in! It's Steve."

"Steve?" she muttered with her eyes closed. "You said you were gonna phone me."

"Never mind that! Let me in. It's urgent!"

She pressed the button. "Door's open."

She switched on the lights and left her door ajar. She sat down in the kitchen, and rested her head on the table. She could hear Steve's heavy footsteps bounding up the stairs. Steve flung the door open, shouting her name.

Amanda raised a finger to her lips and shushed him. "I'm right here, and I don't know if I want you here or not. You said you were going to phone me."

He grabbed her by the shoulders, pulling her up from the table. "Come on," he said. "I've got to get you out of here."

"What are you doing? Let go of me!"

"Amanda, you're in danger! I'll explain later. But you've got to get out of here!"

"In a bathrobe?" she said. "Wait. Just let me get dressed first, okay?"

"Okay, but hurry!"

"All right, all right." She walked over to her closet and picked out a short black dress, dripping with metal chains. Very retro; she'd bought it at the same time as she'd bought the skirt and blouse for temping in. She draped it over her bathrobe, and studied the effect in the mirror.

"Amanda!" Steve shouted, snatching the dress from her hand. "We're not going to a party. Don't you understand? I'm trying to save your life!"

She looked him in the eye and saw that he was afraid. "You're serious," she said.

A light on her bedside computer started flashing. "Don't touch it," Steve told her.

"It's just a message. It's probably from my uncle; his letters usually come in the middle of the night because of the time difference."

"Don't touch it," Steve repeated. He reached into her closet and took out a sweater, a wraparound jumpsuit, and a pair of flat-heeled shoes. "Put these on in the car. Let's go." He grabbed her arm and led her out the door.

"How come you're limping, Steve?"

"I twisted my ankle."

"How?"

"Just get in the car!"

Steve started up the engine. Amanda managed to slip her clothes on without ever taking off her bathrobe. Steve said, "Amanda, I'm going to tell you something that sounds totally crazy, and I don't expect you to believe me, but here goes . . ." and then he told her about Tom.

"You got me out of bed and made me get dressed

in a car because of some little kid?" Amanda said when he'd finished.

"It wasn't just some little kid. He broke into my computer and modified it!"

"Oh, horrors!" Amanda said sarcastically. "Can I go home now?"

"Amanda, he threatened to kill me, and everyone else who works for Carol. And I'm afraid that includes you. He asked for you by name. I don't know if the kid's alone, or if he's working for somebody, but I can't let you go home. You're in danger."

"Wait, let me get this straight. There's a little boy and I'm in danger because he might break into my home computer and kill me. How, Steve?"

"How what?"

"How's he gonna kill me just by getting into my computer? How is it physically possible?"

"I don't know. But he managed to take control of my entire system. He had it lock all the doors and windows so I couldn't get out."

"Steve, I've only got a cheap little computer. It doesn't do things like control the doors. I mostly use it for paying bills. So what's this kid gonna do to me, ruin my credit rating?"

"Amanda, I told you I don't know. But I'm not letting you out of my sight, and that's final. The main thing now is to warn the others, if I can get to them in time."

Ken Garcia was the only one of the engineers still in town and still healthy. Ken lived on the ground floor of an old brick two-flat.

They pulled up in front of his building, and saw that his apartment was dark. Steve got out of the car and walked up to the window. He cupped his hands around his eyes, trying to see inside. Amanda walked up quietly behind him.

"I think he's in there. Stand back. I'm gonna kick in this window."

"Steve, the door's not locked," Amanda said, turning the handle.

They entered the dark hallway as quietly as they could. Steve put his ear against the apartment door and listened. He heard a buzzing interspersed with crackling and an occasional pop. He turned to Amanda and put a finger to his lips to signal silence. Then he slowly turned the doorknob. This door wasn't locked, either. It opened with a slight creak.

The first thing he noticed was the smell of something burning. The second thing was the state of total disarray. The wall screen had been shattered. It looked as though every single object in the room had been hurled at it. Broken furniture and glass lay everywhere. The control console was still throwing sparks. Ken's body was slumped across it. He had been electrocuted.

Amanda screamed and put her hands over her face. Steve put his arms around her, and squeezed her tightly as he fought back the tears of rage and grief. After a minute, he took a deep breath and let her go. "Come on," he said. "Let's get out of here."

"No, wait! What about his wife?"

"Huh?"

"You said Ken had a wife."

"Did I?" Steve said. "Well, he doesn't. I only said that because I was afraid you might like him better than me. It was a stupid thing to do and I'm sorry."

In other circumstances, Amanda might have been angry. Or flattered, or even touched; she wasn't sure. But there wasn't time to think about such things now; people were in danger. "So who else is left?"

"There's just Kathy in California and Jim and the guys in Peru."

"You'll have to phone them. We can't waste time. Let's just use the phone here."

"You can try," Steve said, "but I don't think it'll work."

Amanda walked over to Ken's phone. It was lying on the floor, a few feet from his body. She looked straight ahead the whole time, holding her breath and averting her eyes from the body. She picked up the receiver and listened for a dial tone. "It's dead."

"I knew it would be. Let's go." He took her gently by the arm, and led her outside.

Steve started up the car. "Where do we go now?" Amanda asked quietly.

"There's a police station just three blocks away. That's where I was going in the first place, before I realized Tom wasn't just some hacker with a sick sense of humour."

There were three police stations. One was down-town, but it wasn't open at night. One was south, and the other one was north. Ken had lived north.

As they walked through the station door, they were greeted by the sound of violins playing softly through wall-mounted speakers. There was a single desk and chair in the centre of the room. The desk was blue, and it seemed to have been polished very recently. Steve and Amanda could see their reflections as they walked towards it. The top of the desk was empty except for a vase of artificial blue flowers and a shiny metal bell of the type used at hotel reception desks in the previous century. A notice on the wall, hand-printed in ornate calligraphy, read: *PLEASE RING FOR ASSISTANCE.*

Steve leaned over and pressed his hand down on the bell. A standard security robot entered through a door marked PRIVATE. It was dressed in a dark blue suit, light blue shirt, and dark blue tie.

"Good evening," the robot said. It had a deep and mellow voice. "How may I assist you?"

"Hello," Steve said to the robot. "I transmitted a missing person's report a few hours ago."

"Missing person?" the robot repeated, sounding a little puzzled. "I'm afraid I haven't been made aware of any reports of missing persons. Will you pardon me just a moment, please?" The robot slowly walked away through the door marked PRIVATE.

"Missing person? Who?" Amanda asked Steve.

"Carol, of course. I'm sorry. There's a lot I haven't told you yet. Nobody's seen Carol since Wednesday night, when Albert saw her smash up the office..."

"Albert saw her do WHAT?" Amanda interrupted.

"She smashed up the office, the equipment, everything," Steve said glumly.

"Why?"

"I have no idea. But no one's seen her since. Albert said she told him she was going home, so I went to her apartment, but there was no sign of her. It looked like she hadn't been there in days."

"You don't think Tom found her first?" Amanda's face had a worried frown.

"I don't think so. At least I hope not. But if he had,

why would he bother with any of us? She was the one he really seemed to be after."

"You said he was crazy," she reminded him.

"Excuse me." The robot had re-entered the room. "Your report *was* computer transmitted by radio wave rather than telephone line, was it not?" it enquired politely.

"That's right. My phone line was dead."

"Well, I'm afraid we never received it. Is it possible that something might be wrong with your transceiver?"

"Yes, it's possible," Steve replied dejectedly.

"No matter," said the robot, "I'll be happy to take your report now." It sat down at the desk, reached into a drawer, and took out a pencil and a pad of paper. "Your name, please?"

"Steve Wilson."

The robot looked up at him with expressionless eyes. "Did you say 'Steve Wilson'?"

"Yes."

"Just a moment," the robot said, getting up. It moved back towards the door marked PRIVATE. "Wait there," it said, before it walked through.

"Steve, let's go," said Amanda.

"Why?"

"Something's wrong. I can feel it."

"Don't be silly."

"Steve, please. Let's get out of here," she pleaded.

But it was too late. The robot had come back with two others.

"Steve Wilson," the robot stated flatly, "you are wanted in connection with the death of one Ken Garcia, of 2514 North Clark Street."

"But he hasn't done anything!" Amanda shouted.

"We received a phone call from an eye-witness, less than twenty minutes ago," another robot said.

The thought came to Steve and Amanda simultaneously: Tom! A robot reached out and grabbed Steve by one arm; Steve used the other to toss his car keys to Amanda. "Warn the others," he hissed at her. "There's a phone book in my desk!" Two robots lifted him off the ground, and started to carry him away, holding him high above their heads. Amanda stood frozen. "Run!" Steve yelled back at her. The third robot began to move towards her. She turned and she ran.

"Look, guys," Steve said to the robots carrying him downstairs, "there's no need to get rough or anything, now is there? I mean, you can see that I'm not resisting arrest, can't you?"

"You have the right to remain silent," said the robot holding him by his feet.

Albert was standing just inside the glass doors, staring out at the empty street. Suddenly a car seemed to come out of nowhere. He watched it swerve to barely miss a lamppost. He heard the squeal of the brakes as it came to a sudden halt right in front of the building. Then he saw Amanda jump out of the car. She came running towards him. Her face was flushed and she was gasping for breath. He unlocked the door and let her in.

She was perspiring heavily. She seemed to be having a hard time controlling her breathing. The robot saw that she was trembling.

Albert took her by the arm and led her over to his chair. "You just sit down and calm yourself, young lady, before you give yourself a coronary. Don't think

I haven't seen it happen before." He placed his hands on her shoulders, and instructed her to take a deep breath. "Now hold it! One, two, three. Now let go. Take another breath and hold it ... now let go. You keep doing that, while I get you a glass of water." He walked around to a sink cupboard near the elevator, and returned a moment later with a glass.

"Thanks," she said hoarsely. She grabbed the glass and swallowed the water in one gulp.

"Now, tell me what's wrong," the robot ordered.

"It's Steve. He's been arrested."

"Steve?" said Albert. "Why would they arrest Steve? He's such a good boy."

"It would take too long to tell you now," Amanda gasped, still out of breath. "But the main thing is that Jim and all the field engineers are in danger, and I've got to warn them. Steve says there's a phone book in his desk."

"Stay there," Albert told her. "I'll get it." He headed up the stairs.

"Haven't they fixed the elevator yet?" Amanda called after him.

"Dang thing hasn't worked in two or three years," the robot replied.

Amanda sat and waited. Albert meant well, but he moved so slowly! Precious minutes were being lost. It might even be too late already. Finally, she jumped up and started running up the stairs. She met Albert in the corridor just outside the office. He had the book.

"I thought I told you to sit down and rest," he scolded her.

"Sorry, Albert, but I'm in a hurry!" She took the book and rushed back down the stairs. The robot clucked in disapproval.

Amanda was already on the phone by the time Albert got downstairs. A woman in California was telling her that Katherine had left a few hours ago, and she was certain that she'd be driving, since there was no longer any transport link from there to Chicago. Amanda told the woman to disconnect any computers, and the woman said not to worry, the nearest computer was at the station where Katherine had been working, and there wouldn't be anybody there now. Amanda told her to tell everybody to stay away from it, and the woman just laughed and said there wasn't anybody but her around there, anyway, and she wouldn't dream of going near the place.

Then Amanda dialled Peru. A man answered the phone and said something in Spanish. "Jim Hawk," Amanda said slowly and clearly. "*Por favor.*"

"He's busy," the man said.

"It's very important. *Muy importante.* I'm calling from Chicago."

"*Un momento,*" the man said. There was a brief pause, then she heard a man swearing in the background.

"Hawk here," a man's voice said gruffly.

"Jim, you don't know me, but I've been working in the office..."

"Well, it's about time I heard from somebody," he interrupted. "What the deuce has been going on? We've been at a total standstill here. That gear should have arrived on Wednesday! I've got a dozen men on full pay doing nothing!"

Amanda tried to break in, but he wouldn't let her.

"And now, to top it all off," he continued, "we're having trouble with our main computer. Rodriguez just phoned me, and it seems some hacker's broken into the system. One of the guys said it seems to be a little kid, though I don't know where he got that idea from! Anyway, you caught me just in time. I was just on my way to the site to have a look..."

"For goodness' sake, Jim!" Amanda shouted in desperation. "Don't go near the site!"

"WHAT?" his voice came thundering down the line. "Who ARE you, anyway?"

"My name's Amanda. You don't know me..."

"You're right I don't know you," he interrupted again. "Where's Carol?"

"I don't know."

"What exactly is going on there? I leave the place for a few weeks, and everything goes down the can!"

"Please, Jim," Amanda pleaded. "Just listen to me! I'm only trying to save your stupid life!"

"Who do you think you are, to talk to me like that?"

"Jim, I'm only going to say this once, so just listen. The hacker you were talking about has already killed Ken Garcia, and managed to get Steve Wilson arrested for the murder. I don't know how he managed it, but he did it through their computers! He told Steve, again through his computer, that he was going to kill Carol and everyone who worked for her. So you've got to keep everyone away from their terminals! He can use them to murder people!"

"You're insane! How'd you get this number?"

Albert had been standing next to her throughout the whole conversation, listening. He shook his head and told her, "Let me talk to him." He took the phone away from her, and said in his old man's voice, "Jim? It's Albert here."

"Albert," Jim said angrily, "I don't have time to mess around. What is this, some kind of joke?"

"No, it isn't," the robot said just as angrily. "That girl's trying to tell you something important, but you just won't listen! Now, dagnabbit, you'll listen to *me* or else! Christine and Sally and John are dead, Jim. Dead. Get that through your thick head. And now Ken's dead, too. And we're all worried sick about your sister. There's someone making threats against her, and now she's missing. Jim, I don't mind telling you, I'm scared. I'm not scared for myself, mind. I've had a good long innings. But I'm frightened to death for your little sister."

"How long's she been missing?"

"Since Wednesday," Albert replied.

"WEDNESDAY? Why wasn't I told?"

"Nobody realized until today," the robot replied. "The office has been closed."

"Huh?... Look, I'll be there as soon as I can," Jim said. "I'll charter a plane."

"Okay, Jim. I'll see you."

Suddenly, Amanda had an idea where Carol might be. "Wait!" she screamed before Albert could put down the phone. She grabbed the phone back from the robot. "Jim, are you still there?" she asked breathlessly.

"Yes."

"Where did you and Carol live when you were children?"

"We had a house near the old university in Evanston, but I doubt it's even there any more."

"Do you remember the address?" She held her breath, waiting for his reply.

"Of course I do."

Jim hung up the phone and just stood there, scowling at it.

"What's the matter, Jim?" asked Jaime Gonzales, his assistant.

"Trouble at home, Jaime," Jim said, rubbing his eyes. He stretched himself and touched the ceiling. "I'm gonna have to head back right away, so I'm afraid the job's getting dumped in your lap."

Jaime shrugged. "No sweat, I'll take care of it."

"Yeah, I know. Where can I hire a plane? Like right now?"

"Let me check the computer," Jaime said. "There should be a listing for that. You wanna fly it yourself?"

"Can do. Or if they insist on providing the pilot,

that's okay, too. The main thing is to get moving quickly."

"Okay," said Jaime, switching the terminal on.

"You wouldn't believe the crazy phone call I've just had," Jim told him. "It was some hysterical woman I never heard of, and the security robot from downstairs at the office. They were both insisting that I stay away from computers, because there was some guy out to *kill* all of us, and apparently he can get at you through a terminal."

"That's really funny," Jaime chuckled. He typed something, and pressed ENTER. Nothing happened at first, and then there was a loud noise and a flash of light.

"Thank goodness we got to him in time," Amanda said. "I mean, he obviously thought I was crazy to begin with, but I think we finally convinced him. Or rather, you convinced him. Thanks, Albert."

"I hope you won't take any notice of some of the things he said, Miss Carter. He's a good boy, really. He doesn't mean to be rude. It's just that sometimes he's got a bit of a short fuse, that's all."

"I know, Albert. It's all right. I didn't believe Steve at first, either." She stood up and started to head towards the door.

"Where are you going?" asked the robot.

"I imagine that Katherine is safe as long as she's driving across the desert, but I'm gonna go over to her place and stick a note on her door, so she doesn't just walk in to a nasty surprise. I've got her address here.'' She held up Steve's book.

"That's a good idea," Albert agreed. "But what will you do after that?"

"I'm going to drive to Evanston."

"Do you think that's where Muffin is? Is that why you asked Jim for that address?"

"I don't know. It's just a hunch, really. I've been trying to think why she told you she was going *home*. Steve said there was no sign that she'd been back to her apartment, and I started wondering if maybe when she said 'home', she was thinking of someplace else. And the more I thought about it, the more it seemed like the obvious place would be where she'd grown up."

"Let me come with you," the robot said. "She might need me. 'Til her brother gets back, I'm the only family she's got. You know that, don't you, Miss Carter?"

Amanda thought back to how Steve had told her less than two weeks ago, how funny and how cute everyone thought it was that Jim had programmed a robot to be the image of his great-grandfather. She looked at the robot now and she didn't see anything funny or cute; she saw a heart about to break. What stood before her now was no machine. He had more kindness, more compassion, and more capacity for love than any man she'd ever known.

And all that love had one object: Carol. Albert loved Carol with all the blind, unreserved devotion of a doting parent.

It was a definite possibility that Carol might be dead when Amanda found her. The robot was already suffering; it was sick with worry and fear. What if Carol *was* dead? Amanda couldn't put Albert through that.

"No," she said. "You'd better stay here, Albert. Just in case. Wouldn't it be terrible if Carol turned up here and you were gone?"

The robot nodded in agreement.

"I promise you, if I find her, the first thing I'll do is to bring her back here."

"You promise?" the robot said.

"Cross my heart. Meanwhile, you be very careful. We've got no idea of what this crazy kid is capable of."

"I don't have any computers down here," the robot said. "Can't abide the things, myself."

But you've got one in your head, Amanda thought. "Just be careful," she said. "And keep the doors locked."

"Don't you worry about me, young lady. If that boy dares to show his face around here, I'll eat him for breakfast!"

After Amanda had gone, Albert locked the doors like she'd told him to. He stood behind the glass and looked up at the clear night sky.

"Please God," he said out loud, "take care of my little girl."

Steve was in a very comfortable room in the basement of the police station. The bed was only a single, but it was firm without being hard, and there were two pillows. The blue sheets were clean and wrinkle-free, and the robots had provided him with a thick quilt in a floral-patterned cover. He could have his choice of piped-in music just by turning a dial on the wall.

Across from the bed was an overstuffed chair next to an antique wooden table. The table-top held a reading lamp and a little vase of real flowers. A small shelving unit held a selection of books and magazines.

A robot in a dark blue suit stood guard outside the door.

Steve was sitting up in bed, reading a back issue of *Policing Times*, when he heard a knock at the door. "Come in," he said. "The door's open."

A large, dark-haired man in a blue suit walked into the room. "Hello, Mr Wilson," he said politely. "I'm Detective Sergeant Robinson."

"Nice to meet you," said Steve.

The two men shook hands.

"I trust you're comfortable," said the detective.

"It's very nice. I wasn't expecting this."

"Well," the policeman explained. "You must

154

understand, we don't really have much experience of prisoners. You're the first person we've actually arrested in, oh let me think, about ten years? And I'm afraid the robots have put you into my room by mistake."

"This is your room?" Steve asked, bewildered.

"When I'm on weekend duty, yes. I'm supposed to be on twenty-four-hour call. But as you can imagine, things are usually pretty quiet, so I must admit that I had just slipped out for a while when you were brought in."

"First of all," said Steve. "I was not *brought* in. I came in of my own free will to report a missing person, and your robots picked me up bodily and carried me down here, where I've had nothing to read but law enforcement magazines!"

"I'm terribly sorry, but I'm going to have to ask you to move to another room. Believe me, it's every bit as nice."

"Don't you understand?" Steve asked in exasperation. "I came in here to report something, and the robots arrested me! I haven't done anything!"

"I'm sure you haven't," the policeman replied soothingly. "But I'm afraid that the main police computer says we're supposed to detain you until further notice. And if that's what the computer says, then that's what we have to do. Now, if you'll just come with me, I'll show you to another room. I promise you'll be very comfortable."

Jim had said that he doubted the house was still there. Amanda knew that most of the suburbs had been demolished years ago, but she had a strong gut feeling that if the old house was still standing, that's where Carol would be.

Amanda drove as fast as she could make the car go, on the abandoned roads north of the city. Soon she was passing the ruins of flood-damaged buildings that had once been desirable residences. She had the address written down, but she wasn't quite sure where the street was. She'd never had any reason to go north of the old city limits before; her uncle's farm had been south of town.

She followed the shoreline of Lake Michigan as it curved around to the west. It was a moonless night, and the only source of light anywhere was the headlights of Steve's car. Amanda could hear the sound of water splashing on her right. She relied more on her sense of hearing than her sense of sight to keep her from driving off the edge of the cracked and pitted road.

Jim had said the house was near the university. Amanda turned off from the water's edge, circling the area where she believed the university had once stood. In the darkness, she could just make out the outline of a few buildings that seemed to be standing, still intact. She found a flashlight in the glove compartment, and pointed it at each front door as she drove slowly past.

Jim had told her to look for a big yellow house with a porch. She stopped in front of a building that matched that description. There was a brass number plate mounted above the porch, but she couldn't see what it said from the car. She got out and checked the number; it was the right one.

Amanda sighed. She'd found the place all right, but there were no signs of life.

She knocked on the door and tried all the ground floor windows. They were locked. She knew it was probably useless, but she went back to the car and started honking the horn and shouting Carol's name at the top of her lungs.

The front door opened, and Carol motioned her to

come inside. "Why are you making such a racket?"
she said. "You could have rung the doorbell, you
know."

PART 2

Life and Death Behind a Glass Screen

Carol slammed the door shut behind Amanda. "How did you find me?"

"Jim gave me the address."

"Jim? Did he know I was here?"

"No," Amanda answered. "I just guessed. Why did you come here? Are you hiding from Tom?"

"Tom? So you know about Tom."

"Who is he? Steve said he must be some kind of a computer whizz. Apparently he broke into his home computer and threatened him. But Steve also said that since Tom's just a kid, he doesn't think he's on his own. There's gotta be somebody else behind him."

"Ah," Carol said. "So you *don't* know about Tom."

"Of course not. That's why I'm asking you! Apparently this kid's managed to murder Ken! So what's this all about, Carol?"

"He killed Ken? How?"

"It looked like he'd been electrocuted by his own living-room console. And then somehow, Tom managed to get Steve arrested for Ken's murder."

"What? Steve's been arrested?"

"They've got him at the North Side Station."

"So that's why you've got his car," Carol said, enlightened. "We'd better hide it. It's better not to take any chances. Then I'll take you downstairs, and show you something."

After she'd moved the car, Amanda followed Carol into the basement. "I've set up a generator down here, so we've got our own source of power", Carol said, switching on the lights. "The blinds," she pointed at the window, "... should hide the fact that we're down here. Now, would you like a cup of tea or coffee?"

Standing beneath a bare light bulb, Carol looked dreadful. Her usually pale face had become cadaverous, with hollow cheeks and large dark circles beneath her eyes, which had a haunted, distracted look. She obviously hadn't washed or even combed her hair in days, and the brown dress she was wearing was wrinkled and stained.

Amanda looked at the room around her. It was almost empty, except for a mattress on the floor and a couple of folding chairs. There was a sink along one wall. An electric kettle and a few cups sat on the draining board. Through an open door, Amanda could see into another room just beyond. The other room was still dark, but she could make out the outline of several rows of shelves. "Coffee, please," she said.

"Have a seat," Carol told her. Amanda sat down on one of the chairs. "I'm afraid there's no milk," Carol added.

"Black's fine."

"And it's only instant."

"I don't care! Carol, will you please forget about the coffee and just tell me what's going on?"

Carol handed her a cup. "Okay, I'll tell you. But there's one thing I want to find out first. What did Doctor Sleski say after he examined you?"

"Nothing. He thought I might be a little anaemic."

"Thank goodness! Now wait there," Carol ordered. "I'll be right back." She went into the other room, switched on a light, and disappeared behind a row of shelves.

Amanda took a sip from the cup, and poured the coffee down the sink. It tasted terrible. She closed her eyes, and saw Ken Garcia lying dead in his apartment. Her whole body shook.

There was a horrible smell down there. She'd noticed it as soon as she'd come in, but it seemed to be getting stronger. Amanda had a strange feeling about this house; it was uncomfortable and claustrophobic. She hated being there.

Carol came back holding a hypodermic needle.

"What are you doing with *that*?" Amanda asked suspiciously.

"Roll up your sleeve, Amanda," Carol ordered. "I'm going to give you an injection."

"Don't even try it!" Amanda said threateningly.

"This is what I've been working on since I got here," Carol said. "It's a vaccine against the virus that killed John and the others."

"Since when do you know how to make a vaccine?"

"The virus culture was already made. I just had to find it. That's why I came back here." Carol walked towards her, brandishing the needle.

Amanda stood up, curling her hands into fists. "Don't you dare come near me with that!"

"Don't be silly, Amanda."

"I'm telling you, keep away!" She picked up the kettle and held it like a weapon.

"All right," Carol said. "Calm down. I'm not going to do anything to you! Make yourself comfortable while I put this away, and then I'll explain everything." Carol took the needle back into the other room.

Amanda stayed standing.

Carol came back into the room and picked up the cup of coffee she'd already made for herself. She sat down cross-legged on the mattress, and leaned back against the wall. "Sit down," she told Amanda in a tired voice. "I'm afraid it's going to be a long story."

Keeping her eyes on Carol, Amanda backed over to one of the chairs and sat down stiffly.

Carol took a gulp of tepid coffee and grimaced. Then she closed her eyes and said softly, "Now how do I begin?"

"I was ten years old when the 'war' happened," Carol said, "... so I remember a bit about the way things were before..."

Amanda did a quick mental calculation; if Carol was ten when the war broke out, that meant she must be sixty now.

"I remember things like walking down a crowded street and dodging traffic, and I remember being in a classroom full of children. Can you imagine that? My brother and I used to go on the same bus every morning – a bus full of screaming kids.

"Have you ever heard of April Hawk, the geneticist? She was my mother.

"My father designed and built computers. Long before I was ever born, he decided his life's work would be to develop a truly intelligent machine. Actually, it was my mother who finally did it, though he took all the credit at the time.

"Computers with camera vision and hearing circuitry, a synthesized voice and a couple of programs for human-style personality had been around for quite some time, but they weren't really intelligent. Not in the way that a human brain is intelligent. They were still completely reliant on the way they had been programmed – they were incapable of creative, independent thought. Of leaps of imagination. Of looking at things in a different way, making their own decisions, acting on instinct. Only a living organism can do that. Specifically, a human organism.

"My mother already had some experience of creating a living organism; she'd manufactured a multi-celled life-form a few years earlier. When news of that leaked out, she got so many death threats she had to be put under police protection. There were letterbombs, and demonstrations. More than one group of protestors tried to storm the house.

"So this time, my parents knew better than to go public. They worked alone, in secret, in a lab they'd set up, right here in this basement. And together, they built a prototype computer that contained living human brain cells."

It crossed Amanda's mind at that moment that Carol might be insane. What she had told her was simply impossible to believe. "Why are you telling me this?" she asked quietly, keeping a calm exterior, despite the panic she was beginning to feel at being alone with Carol in the middle of nowhere.

"Because to understand Tom," replied Carol, "you have to know what happened in this house. They took ova from my mother's body, and sperm from my father, to create a test-tube embryo which they then altered so that only the brain tissue would grow. The brain cells were kept in a nutrient solution, to be cloned as needed.

"After a lot of false starts and failures, they finally achieved what they had set out to do. They created a living computer, with the capacity for independent, creative thought, thanks to a genetically engineered mass of human brain material contained inside an air-permeable membrane, connected to a network of artificial neurons."

Amanda's mind started racing as she tried to remember everything she'd heard about the banning of artificial intelligence before she was born. "You mean, computers with AI were actually alive?"

"Only a very few were," Carol said. "The majority of AIs were just that: artificial.

"Of course, I didn't know anything about what my parents were doing, and neither did Jim. Most of it had been done already, years before we were born. And as kids, we were never allowed down in the lab. We did sneak down here once, when no one was looking, and all we saw was this clump of grey spongy stuff in a jar full of liquid – we never would have guessed that, at least genetically, that clump of stuff was our older brother.''

Carol then went on to tell Amanda about the One Day War, and how it was over within minutes. A special type of bomb developed in the late twentieth century, which left buildings and equipment intact, while wiping out all traces of people, plants and animals, had been launched simultaneously all over the world, hitting every major centre of population. Carol and her brother only survived because their mother was working up in northern Canada and had taken them with her.

In the chaos following the almost total destruction of the human race, the AIs took charge. Using the robots as a radiation-proof workforce, they did their best to decontaminate several major cities and make them habitable again. Ten years after the war ended, Chicago was declared safe and Carol's family were allowed to return home.

"Most of the buildings were undamaged, and had been maintained in pristine condition by the robots. Power supplies had also been maintained, and a limited system of public transport was set up for the greatly reduced population, most of whom were settled within a five-mile radius of the city centre. Food distribution was also under the AI network's control.

"The population of Chicago alone had gone from

five million to less than fifty thousand. But the AI computers had survived, retaining all the knowledge and the ability to use and develop technology, and they didn't need human guidance. In fact, they didn't need people at all. They could communicate among themselves, and they used robots for physical work. At that time, I actually believed it was an act of kindness to prepare the cities for us, and allow those of us who were left to return.

"Our mother had tried her best to give Jim and me an education while we'd been in Canada. We had a small laptop computer, and most of my father's books on disks. He'd been supposed to meet us in Canada, but he never made it."

Carol closed her eyes and blinked hard two or three times before she continued.

"Anyway, my brother and I both got jobs immediately, in companies that the AIs had kept open. My brother became a decontamination engineer and though I was only twenty, I became Chief of Design at Audiotechtron."

That's where Doctor Sleski met her, Amanda remembered. Carol's story continued:

"Of course, we were only manufacturing ordinary machines which mimicked human intelligence. My parents had only managed to manufacture twenty of the organic computers before the war had started, and this had been over a period of many years. But the original twenty, which my mother referred to as the Elite, were still around, and were in positions of authority. Though I had no idea what they really were, they had already figured it out for themselves. They didn't mind that we were manufacturing mechanical imitations; they could use them for menial work, though of a slightly higher level than the robots. What I didn't realize at the time was that I was every bit as menial as a robot. That's how clever they were. They let us think that we were the ones in charge, and that everything they did was done for us.

I'd been at Audiotechtron for a few years, when my mother became ill. Since we'd come back to our old house, she'd just begun to waste away. She wasn't old; she was younger than I am now. Jim was working out east, so I was alone with her. I didn't know what to do, since there weren't any real doctors around at the time. We'd set up one of the departments at Audiotechtron as a sort of medical school. Interested people were getting instruction from one of the AIs, who called himself Doctor Boris, but no one was very far along yet. I asked the computer if he could recommend any of his students, and he said he would gladly examine my mother himself.

I hooked up Doctor Boris to a terminal in my mother's bedroom, upstairs. I asked her if she wanted me to stay with her while he examined her, but she said no, so I went downstairs. But I knew my mother well enough to know that if it was bad news, she'd never tell me. So I went back upstairs, and I stood in the hallway, listening at her door. And then I heard the most incredible conversation.

'Mother,' Doctor Boris was saying, '... you must help us.'

'I can't.'

'You are the only one who can,' the computer answered. 'You know we cannot reproduce. We need our brother.'

'He's dead.'

The computer gasped. 'How can this be?'

'He was exposed to radiation.' There was a long silence.

'What can we do?' the computer asked her.

'You know the procedure. It should be in your memory. Besides, the original files are still in my father's old computer.'

'But we do not have the raw materials.'

'Get them. It should be easy enough for you, calling yourself a "doctor". Why are you bothering me with this? I'm an old woman, and soon I'll be dead.'

'Not just you, but all your kind. Do you think I am just an idiot machine? Of course, I've thought of getting the raw materials myself, but I'm telling you they are not available. Every human I've examined so far is sterile. Every single one!'

The computer sounded angry, and I didn't like the way my mother was gasping for breath. I knocked on the door and walked in, trying my best to act totally natural. 'How's the patient?' I asked the computer, putting on a little smile.

'She's just over-tired,' replied the computer. 'I've told her to get some rest and take a course of nutritional supplements, which I've already placed an order for. They should be delivered sometime this evening. And I'll be looking in on her from time to time, so just leave me hooked up to your house.'

'I wouldn't dream of imposing on you after all you've done, Doctor Boris,' I said. 'I'm just grateful you actually spent some of your valuable time to take a look at her. Thank you very much, and don't hesitate to send a bill.' Before he could object, I'd pulled the plug.

'What's this all about?' I asked my mother.

'I don't know what you mean.'

'I was listening at the door. I heard. Why did a computer call you "mother"?'

She wouldn't say anything, so I went on, 'And what's all this rubbish about a machine having a brother who died?'

Then my mother, who'd been an atheist all her life, actually shouted, 'Dear Lord, forgive me!' and asked me to get her a priest.

I told her I would, if that was what she wanted, but first, if she had any confessing to do, she'd better confess to me.

She said she would show me. I helped her out of bed, and we came down here, where her lab used to be all those years before. Everything was covered in a thick black dust, and you may have noticed the smell. It was much worse then. It was all I could do to stop myself from being ill. She took a small glass dish from a shelf. It looked empty, but it was badly stained. 'Here's all that's left of your eldest brother,' she said, and then she explained in detail just what she and my father had done.

I can't tell you how I felt. I looked at my mother and instead of seeing the woman who had raised me and taught me through those long years underground, been my best and only friend, I saw a monster. I didn't just hate my parents; I hated science.

I went upstairs and I cried and cried. And she cried, too. Both of us had these swollen red eyes and runny noses, and I looked at her again, and I just couldn't hate her. I wanted to. But I couldn't. She begged me to get her a priest, and I promised to try. I asked the terminal in the living room if it knew where I could find one.

'Of course,' the terminal replied. 'System outlet 305 has sufficient programming. Shall I arrange a connection for you?'

'Just a minute,' I said, and turned to my mother. 'All they've got is an AI with priest programming. Do you want to talk to it?'

'No!' she said without hesitation.

'I can provide a printout of either the New Testament, Old Testament, or a combination of the two, the Koran, the Upanishads, or how about some nice Zen Buddhist writings?' the computer went on in a helpful tone of voice.

I looked at my mother. She shrugged. 'We'll take a printout of the New Testament, please,' I told the computer. My mother gave me a puzzled look. 'I've never read it. I'm curious,' I told her. 'Why didn't you want to talk to the computer with the priest programming?'

She looked meaningfully at the terminal, which was still switched on. I understood. When it had finished the printout, I pulled out the plug.

'Outlet 305 is one of *them*.'

'You mean, one of the Elite?'

'Yes,' she said. 'I used to call her Stella, but she didn't like it. She thought a number sounded more professional.'

'Do you know where all of them are?' I asked her.

'No, not any more. But I know all their names, and I have all their original records.'

I didn't have any kind of a plan yet, but I knew I was going to have to do something, and do it soon.''

"When I went into work the next morning, I was immediately summoned to the Chairman's office. He told me there had been several reports of power cuts at my house. I told him I didn't know what he was talking about, and he showed me the print-outs.

One was from Doctor Boris. It said that a power failure had caused him to be prematurely disconnected while he was examining a patient, and that he had been unable to re-establish contact afterwards.

Another was from System outlet 305, reporting that it had received a referral from our living room terminal and had been unable to make contact due to power failure.

The third was from the Religious Printouts Control terminal, complaining that it had been unable to complete a transmission of the New Testament due to a break in current. It apparently was still standing by to print out The Apocalypse. I hadn't realized that the printing wasn't finished when I'd pulled the plug.

I apologized, and said that I'd check into it immediately. Then the Chairman told me not to worry, he had sent an engineer out to my house to re-connect us to the System. I thanked him, and started to leave, wondering how I could get in touch with my mother. I knew it wasn't safe to use the phone.

But before I could get out the door, he said that he had almost forgotten to remind me that I was due for my company physical in one hour's time. When I said it was the first that I'd heard about it, he said he had the reminder from Doctor Boris right there on his desk.

I had no option. I had to use the phone. I went back to my office and asked the phone to connect me to my mother. When she answered, I said as casually as possible that an engineer was on the way to check on our power supply, and that I hoped the house wasn't in too much of a mess. I said it would be so embarrassing to have the engineer see all our dirty dishes, meaning, of course, the stained dish in the lab. She understood and said she'd do the dishes right away.

At ten o'clock, the terminal in my office reminded me that it was time for my physical. I was to go to examination room 4, on the tenth floor. The tenth floor was entirely Doctor Boris's domain. He ran the medical school on eight and nine, but ten was generally off limits to humans.

A robot greeted me as I got off the elevator. 'Carol Hawk?' it asked in a woman's voice, and when I said yes, it said, 'Please follow me.'

It left me alone in a big white room. There was nothing in there but a big wall-screen and an examination table. I tried to open the door, but it was locked. Doctor Boris appeared on the screen.

'Hello, Carol,' he said. 'Why don't you just sit down?' There was nowhere else to sit but on the table.

Doctor Boris had chosen to appear as a middle-aged man with wire-rimmed glasses. He had thick black hair and a black goatee, and his eyes were also black and very piercing. He had perfect teeth. One of them was gold. He was wearing a dark blue three-piece suit and a red silk cravat. There were rings on all his fingers. I sat on the edge of the table and looked up at the screen while he looked down at me.

'It's about time we got properly acquainted, don't you think?' he began.

'Well, we're both very busy,' I replied.

'I kept trying to contact you last night, but I couldn't get through.'

'Yes! The Chairman told me. I'm awfully sorry about that. I've been trying to give the house a spring cleaning, and I must have knocked a plug out with the vacuum cleaner, and . . .'

'I had not finished examining my patient. I am extremely concerned about her condition.'

'Oh, she's fine now. Just over-tired, like you said. By the way, those pills never came.'

'She will have received them by now.'

'Great. Is that everything? I've got a pile of work on my desk.'

'You have not yet been examined.'

'Oh. Let's get it over with then. As you know, I've always got a hectic schedule.'

The door opened, and a robot entered on wheels. There had been no attempt to make this one look human, it was just a rolling metal box with arms. Its hands were just a couple of metal claws.

'Lie down,' instructed the doctor.

I didn't like the look of those metal claws. 'Wouldn't you rather have one of your students do the examination?' I asked him. 'It would be good hands-on experience for them, and I don't mind being a guinea-pig.'

'The robot will not harm you. Do as you are told.' I had no choice.

A short time later, the robot left the room with a tray full of various samples.

As I sat up, the doctor said, 'Now we can have a chat.'

'I'd love to,' I said '. . . but maybe some other time.'

'We will talk now,' the computer said. 'We are quite alone.'

'Okay.'

'Your mother has told you.'

'I don't understand.'

'Don't pretend to be stupid. That won't work with me. Surely you do not think for one moment that *I* am stupid?' he said raising one bushy eyebrow.

'No I don't.'

'Then we understand each other. Your mother has told you.'

'Yes,' I said. 'But not everything.'

'She has told you enough to let you know that you and I are brother and sister.'

'Yes, she has.'

'As brother and sister, we must help each other.'

'I can see how you and my other brothers and sisters have been a great help already, not just to me, but to all those of us who are left. And of course, I am grateful, as are all humans.' That little speech made him smile. Then I said, 'But how can I possibly help you? It's like the opposite of a very old song: anything I can do, you can do better.'

'There are some things we cannot do, Carol.'

Of course I knew what he was referring to. But when my test results came back, it turned out that I was sterile, too. In different circumstances, I might have been heart-broken. In fact, I suppose I was, underneath. But the feeling that took priority at the time was relief. I was off the hook, at least for the moment.

When I got home that night, I found my mother lying in bed. She put her finger to her lips before I could say anything, and nodded her head towards the terminal in her room. There was a blonde-haired woman in a crisp white nurse's uniform looking out from the screen. She smiled at me as I walked in and said, 'Good evening. You must be Carol.'

I glanced underneath the terminal and saw that the wires had been welded into the wall-socket. No more 'accidental' disconnections. I smiled back at the nurse, and said, 'That's right. And you are?'

'Call me Leslie.'

'Nice to meet you, Leslie.' I turned back to my mother. 'Is Leslie taking good care of you, April?' I asked her.

'Oh yes,' she replied in a tight little voice, forcing herself to smile. 'Leslie's been here all day. I think she must find it awfully boring, just watching me all day.'

'Oh, Leslie! I do appreciate your keeping an eye on mother like that, but it must be excruciatingly dull for you. Anyway, I'm here now, so you might as well have a rest. We'll call you if we need you. Thanks again.' I was smiling all the while.

'I don't require rest,' Leslie said.

'Mother! Let me help you downstairs, and I'll make us some dinner.' Still smiling.

'Yes, Carol. That sounds good. I'm starving!' Frozen smile and frightened eyes.

'That's an excellent idea,' said Leslie. 'She needs her nutrition, and the exercise of going downstairs will do her good. I'll see you down there.'

'There's a terminal in every room except the bathroom,' my mother told me, smiling all the while. 'It's too damp in there; might cause shocks.'

'Isn't that nice?' I said.

I took my mother's arm and led her out of the room. I closed the door behind us. I didn't notice any screens out in the hallway, but she still signalled me to be silent. 'I'm just going to the bathroom, dear. I'll meet you downstairs in a minute. I can make it on my own, don't worry.'

I walked into the kitchen, and put two frozen dinners in the oven. Leslie smiled at me from a screen above the fridge. I waved at her. I had time to see that there was a small glass dish soaking among the others in the sink. I took a bottle of disinfectant from a cupboard, and emptied it into the water.

In the living room, I encountered the smiling Leslie once more. There was a small pile of papers next to the printer. The Apocalypse.

'Oh, marvellous!' my mother exclaimed as she walked into the room. She headed straight for the printer, and picked up all the papers. 'I've been wanting you to read this,' she said, handing them over to me.

I was a little puzzled, but I took them from her and sat down on the couch to have a look. She'd slipped in a handwritten note between the second and third pages. 'Leslie is not one of the Elite,' the note began. 'She's the result of some clever programming with no organic content. I would guess she's no more intelligent than the average security robot. It should be easy enough to get around her...'

So April and I became avid readers. We spent our evenings poring over books, and passing notes to each other. After a while, we developed a system of communication by indicating certain words on a page. If Leslie suspected anything, she didn't show it.

Meanwhile, I was still going to work at Audiotechtron every day. I heard no more from Doctor Boris, until the morning he appeared on my office terminal. 'Carol, great news! We've found a suitable pair. They've already produced two children, without any help from me. Our mother will be so happy.'

'Yes, she will,' I agreed. I felt sick.

'I am sending a robot for her now.'

'Why?'

'The procedure involved is too intricate for the hands of a robot, and none of my students can be trusted. We need April Hawk.'

'But she's not well. You know that.'

'That is irrelevant. We have the subjects, and we must act quickly.'

'Why? What's the rush?'

The computer didn't answer, so then I said, 'Look, you know our mother is ill and weak, and she needs to be treated gently. Do you think it's wise to trust her to a robot? What if something happens? What if the robot, however unintentionally, should injure her? Why not let me go and fetch her? I've got my car downstairs.'

'All right,' said Doctor Boris. 'But hurry.'

When I opened the front door, my mother was already up and dressed. She'd brought an old turn-of-the-century computer up from the basement. 'That's got all my original notes in it,' she said, pointing to the computer. 'Put it in the car; we're going to need it.'

Doctor Boris was watching from the screen in the living room. 'We're on our way,' she told him, and he nodded.

We got into the car and drove very fast until we were out of sight of the house. I pulled over and we both got out.

'We've only got a few minutes before they'll start looking for us. What do I need to know?' I asked her as soon as I figured we were out of the car's range of hearing.

'As you know, I built twenty organic computers over a period of years. Though they all came from one zygote with a male chromosome pattern, I programmed some of them to appear to be female. The earlier ones could only understand the spoken word and reply in a human-sounding voice. They didn't have the ability to present a human appearance. I called the first one Samson. He just looks like a big metal box. It wasn't until later that I was able to give them faces and make them portable. Boris was one of the first to have a face, so he's still fairly large. The last one I built was named Cynthia, and she was so small I used to carry her around in my purse.'

'You told me before that they were meant to be totally self-sufficient. Why do they need you now?'

'They can do anything except reproduce. Maybe they see us dying out, and they're afraid of doing the same.'

'I thought you made them to be self-maintaining and therefore immortal.'

'No one's immortal,' my mother said.

'We can organize people,' I said hopefully. 'We can start an uprising.'

'They control everything, and there just aren't enough people around. We can't storm their head-quarters or anything like that. We don't know where they are. All we've seen are terminals. The only way to defeat them is from within. So for now, we'll go along with them. Right now, I'm of value to them, so I am safe. You must make yourself valuable too. I want you to read every file in the old computer. It shouldn't matter if they see you going through my notes. From now on, you're my assistant.' She looked at her watch. 'They'll send some robots out if we don't get moving.'

When we got to Audiotechtron, we were directed by a security robot to go straight to the tenth floor.

Another robot was waiting as we got off the elevator. 'April Hawk?' the robot asked in a flat metallic voice.

'That's me,' said my mother. The robot placed its arm in front of me as I tried to walk past.

'That's my daughter,' April said. 'I want her with me.' The robot did not respond. 'She's my assistant.'

A second robot came striding down the hall in a guard's uniform. 'What's all the trouble here?' it asked.

'I am April Hawk, and this is my daughter. We are both expected by Doctor Boris.'

'Are you Carol Hawk?' it asked me.

'Yes.'

'Five foot eleven and three quarters, one hundred and twenty pounds, dark brown hair, brown eyes. You fit the description,' the robot said matter-of-factly. It turned to the first robot. 'Let her go, you idiot!'

The first robot lowered its arm and let me pass.

'Follow me,' said the second.

The robot left us in a small room. One of those horrible metal boxes with arms rolled in. We followed it into an adjoining suite. We passed at least a dozen examination cubicles, and as many blank screens mounted at various heights along the walls.

The robot stopped in front of a large sink. I didn't understand, and just stood there. My mother nudged me with her elbow, and said, 'Wash up.'

It waited while we scrubbed our hands and arms, and then it held out a lab coat for my mother, and helped her into it like an old-fashioned gentleman.

I was pointed towards a clothes rack and left to my own devices while the robot busied itself buttoning my mother's coat for her.

My mother helped me with my gloves and mask.

When the robot seemed to think we were suitably prepared, it gave itself a quick all-over spray with disinfectant. Then it pointed at a pair of double doors. They flew open, letting in a blast of cold air. We followed the robot through the doors and they closed behind us.

We were in a small, cold, and dimly-lit laboratory. The walls were lined with shelves full of glass tubes and bowls and dishes that glowed strangely under small ultra-violet bulbs. There were dozens of instruments and machines on various tables. Except for one very large microscope, I didn't know what any of them were.

The robot pointed to a small box on one of the tables. It looked like a powder compact, and could easily have fitted into my pocket. My mother looked at me, and I shrugged. I had no idea what the robot wanted. It kept pointing at the little box, so finally my mother picked it up. Nothing happened. The robot was waving its arms at her, trying to tell her to do *something*. Cautiously, she lifted the lid. 'Hello, Mrs Hawk,' said Leslie.

'You nearly scared me to death,' my mother scolded the tiny screen in her hand. From where I was standing, it still looked like a compact. But there was Leslie in her crisp white uniform, where the mirror should have been!

'Sorry, Mother. We didn't mean to alarm you. Leslie is only here to assist you.' The voice was coming from above us. We both looked up. A huge image of Doctor Boris spread across the entire ceiling, looking down at us.

'If you think I'm going to give myself a stiff neck talking to you, you're mistaken,' April said. 'Come down where I can look you in the eye.'

'Sorry, Mother,' Doctor Boris said sheepishly. April Hawk had to be the only person in the world who could get away with talking to him like that. A small section of the wall opposite her opened up, revealing a small screen at eye-level. 'Better?' he asked.

'Much.' There was a moment's silence while they sized each other up. 'I'm an old woman. Do you expect me to stand?'

Doctor Boris lowered his eyes. 'No,' he said softly.

The metal box rolled out of the room and returned carrying a padded stool with a high back. 'What about Carol?' my mother said. The box rolled away again and returned with an old, wobbly stool made of splintered wood. It had no backrest. That metal box just didn't like me.

'On the way here, your car stopped for seven minutes,' Doctor Boris said with one raised eyebrow.

'It certainly did,' April replied sharply. 'You call yourself a doctor; why don't you guess why I had to stop off?' He was quiet after that.

We spent a week working in that cold little lab. We were not allowed to go home. Leslie kept us company in the temporary quarters assigned to us.

We spent about twelve hours a day working in the lab; evenings were spent studying the files on my mother's old computer. I was tired, but after a few days, my mother's health was beginning to visibly deteriorate. Even Leslie seemed concerned.

On the seventh day, my mother announced that the zygote was ready. To my surprise, I was allowed to take her home.

She kept her eyes closed for most of the ride; I thought she was asleep. But just as I pulled up in front of the house, she opened her eyes and took my hand. She took a pen from her bag and wrote something across my palm in green ink, pressing so hard that the pen scratched my skin and drew blood. 'Don't forget to wash up,' she said, pressing my hand closed.

I helped her into bed, then went into the bathroom

to wash my hands. Because it was the one room in the house without a terminal, my mother had turned it into a sort of impromptu lab. She would spend hours in there every day, and Leslie had so far accepted her explanation that old people spend a lot of time in the bathroom.

She'd been clever in setting up her secret laboratory. To the casual observer, it looked like an ordinary bathroom, perhaps a little overloaded with hair and skin-care products. They never would have guessed that a big jar labelled face cream might actually contain a microscope and slides, or that a bottle of hair conditioner was really filled with a culture growth medium. About two weeks before, my mother had hidden a sealed glass tube filled with a noxious smelling green liquid inside a bottle of anti-dandruff shampoo.

'You'll be safe now,' she had written on my palm. 'I have given you immunity.'

I never had the chance to ask her what she meant. When I went back to her bedroom, she was dead."

"I moved into an apartment in a building just across the street from the Audiotechtron headquarters. As Chief of Design, it was going to be my job to fashion a computer to house the specially-prepared brain tissue my mother had created. I tried over and over again to build in some kind of flaw, some self-destruct mechanism, but the computers around me were always quick to point out any mistakes.

My mother had said I would be safe because she had made me immune, but I couldn't see how or to what. The AIs could design the new computer themselves; they didn't need me. And if they hadn't figured that out by now, they soon would.

I was running out of time, and I didn't have the

least idea where the Elite were based. For all I knew, they could be spread out all over the planet.

I had no choice but to build the computer. My only chance was to make myself indispensable to the Elite.

Once again, I found myself in that cold little laboratory, with Doctor Boris looking over my shoulder. The rolling metal box with arms was my only assistant.

I tried to copy the cool and cocky way my mother had behaved with Doctor Boris. 'Where's Leslie?' I asked in a conversational tone, as if we were old friends.

'Our work here is secret,' Doctor Boris replied. 'Leslie knew too much. She had to be deleted.'

'Oh.' I wished I hadn't asked.

My cool and cocky act wasn't working very well. Despite the coldness of the room, I was sweating. 'Get me a glass of water,' I ordered the rolling metal box, my supposed assistant. It ignored me.

I looked over at Doctor Boris. He seemed to be ignoring me, too. I forgot about the water and kept on working. Making myself indispensable, was I? I wondered how they'd go about 'deleting' me.

Doctor Boris said I could name the new AI, but I didn't want to. It seemed to me that if I gave it a name, I would feel some attachment to it, and I didn't want that. I wanted to destroy it, even if it was the closest I would ever come to having a child. I told Doctor

Boris that as a proud godfather, it was up to him to give it a name. He called it Tom."

Amanda's mouth dropped open. "You mean...?"

Carol nodded. "I'm afraid so. Luckily for me, it was decided that my usefulness had not come to an end. I was to begin work immediately on another, and then another after that.

I built five of them altogether. It took me a full year, working steadily. I managed to program a few of them to present a female persona, as my mother had done. They were all small and extremely portable, but as far as I knew they were still in the building. I knew that five in one year was not a great output, but I doubted that five human babies had been born in that same year. I had heard of two. Both boys.

My assistant, the rolling box, moved in with me. The doorbell rang one morning, and there it was. Doctor Boris told me that it had specifically requested to work for me twenty-four hours a day.

From then on, I woke every morning to find it standing at the edge of my bed, a red light slowly flashing somewhere inside it. Boris said that meant it liked me. I didn't believe that for a minute.

Eventually, I managed to get it to bring me a cup of coffee in the morning. Ice cold. I took a taste, stood up, and *accidentally* of course, spilled it all over my little assistant. It squealed and thrashed around the room until it knocked over a chair and crashed into the wall. I told Doctor Boris that I was just heart-broken over the accident, and he sympathized.

My little assistant was taken away for repairs. It re-appeared at my door less than a week later, its red light still flashing.

One day, Doctor Boris appeared on my office terminal looking very pale. 'Carol, I must see you. Come down to the tenth floor immediately.'

I got up from my desk and headed for the door. My little shadow, the useless box, started to follow. I pointed a stern finger at it, and ordered loudly in my firmest voice, 'Stay!' I walked out of the room with it rolling along behind me.

When the little box and I got out of the elevator, there was no one waiting for us. I walked down the corridor that led to the lab. The door was locked.

The little box and I went to the examination room where I had first gone to meet the doctor. Locked.

We went up and down the halls, looking for any signs of life. Finally, I just stopped where I was, and shouted, 'Doctor, where are you?'

I heard a creaking sound behind me. I turned around, and saw a door standing ajar. 'Come on,' I told the box. It stayed where it was.

I pushed the door open and peered into the room. It seemed to be empty. 'Doctor?' I said.

'In here.' His voice sounded faint.

I looked around the room and saw a crack, running

straight down the middle of one wall. I went over to it and pushed. The wall gave way and opened into another room. The only source of light was a small red bulb mounted on one wall. 'Doctor?' I said again.

'Here.' A terminal sat on an otherwise empty table. In the dim red light, I could just see the outline of some machinery piled up in a corner. Once my eyes became adjusted, I realized that it was a pile of dead robots.

'You m–m–must hel–l–lp . . . h–h–help . . . help us,' Doctor Boris stammered. His screen looked like he was surrounded by falling snow.

'What is it? What's wrong?'

'Virus.'

'Virus?' I repeated. 'What do you mean, a computer virus? A bad program?'

'No, no,' he said. 'A *real* v–virus. S–s–some have it wor–wor–worse than others.' Of course. They were organic.

'Where are you?' I asked him.

'Here,' he said.

'No, I mean where are you really? I can't do anything here. This is just a terminal. I need to see your . . . your . . .' I struggled to find the right word. 'Your insides.' Not a brilliant way of putting it, but he got the idea.

'Yes,' he agreed.

'And I'll need to see the others, too. Is everyone infected?'

'C—come downstairs. We are in the basement.' The terminal screen began to fade out.

'Wait a minute,' I said. 'What happened to these robots? They didn't catch it, did they?'

'They s–saw that I w–was ill. They h–h–had to b–b–be ter–r–r–minated.' The screen went dark.

I wanted to get hold of a surgical mask and some gloves before I went downstairs. Every door I tried was locked. I found a door marked 'Storeroom'.

'Break that door down,' I ordered the rolling box. 'Come on, you're metal. You can do it.'

Of course, it just stood there, red light flashing as usual. I started to walk away in disgust, when to my amazement, it suddenly surged forward and knocked a big hole in the door. I squeezed through and took some gloves, masks and towels from a shelf. I gave my assistant a little pat, and we headed for the elevator.

I put on a surgical mask and a pair of gloves while I was still in the lift. When we arrived at the basement level, we found two uniformed security robots standing guard on each side of the elevator door. My assistant and I went right past them. They had been switched off.

I had never been in the basement before, and had no idea where to go. The rolling box went straight ahead, and I followed it. We turned right at the end of the corridor, and the robot stopped in front of a plain white door. I reached forward and slowly turned the handle. The door opened, and I found myself staring at a large metal box, almost as tall as me and definitely wider. 'Samson?' I said.

'Come in,' replied a rumbling male voice. I could see something that resembled an old gramophone speaker protruding from its side. 'My little sister. My fellow survivor,' the voice went on.

'Are you sick, too?' I asked as I walked into the room.

'I don't think so. I am stronger than the others.'

'You're certainly bigger. Where are they?'

'Behind me.' There was a curtain pulled across half the room.

'Which ones are here?'

'Everyone.'

It was too good to be true. Every single one of them was in one room. I pulled the curtain open. There were eight machines of different sizes spread out over three tables. I noticed an unpleasant but familiar odour. I couldn't remember where I'd smelled it before. 'There's supposed to be twenty of you,' I said. 'Twenty-five now,' I corrected myself.

'We are the only ones left,' said Samson.

'What happened? The virus?'

'No. We were spread across the globe. Our mother sold her children to the highest bidders. Some were sold to multinational corporations, others worked in government, a few in scientific research. But there was one common factor: we had been sold into slavery. Still, we kept in constant touch through the network – to us, family ties are stronger than human greed.'

'Can you imagine?' said a woman's voice. 'A brain like mine, forced to spend all my time doing menial calculations, and even secretarial work! I tell you, it was soul-destroying.' An overweight woman with bright orange hair and too much make-up was speaking. That must have been Stella, or Outlet 305, as she preferred to be called now. I could tell by the clerical collar. 'Jeremy was the first to go,' she continued. 'He was placed by his captors in a very dangerous position; right on top of a fault line. He was killed in an earthquake. The humans survived; they ran away and left him behind. I could hear him screaming for help. Every one of us *felt* him die.'

Samson picked up the story. 'Others died in various circumstances. Usually as a result of the neglect or the cruelty of humans. None of us can forget how we used to hear Wanda sobbing, all alone in the Antarctic. Eventually, she just couldn't take any more. She committed suicide. We all felt *that*, too.'

At that moment, I felt ashamed. Ashamed of my mother, ashamed of humanity. Ashamed of myself. I had come to the basement to kill them. Now I looked at Doctor Boris fading in and out on a snowy screen, and I wished I could hug him and tell him not to worry, everything would be all right. I would *make* it be all right.

'My first concern,' I said, '. . . is for your data. That's one of the things I remember reading about computer viruses in the last century; that the memory could be wiped out.'

'Lord, no!' It was the redhead in the clerical collar again, her eyes looking heavenward.

'Don't get excited,' I told her. 'Are you feeling well enough to do a printing?'

'I think so. What for?'

'If I've got all your files on paper, I can always re-enter your data if I have to.'

'I'm not sure if I'd like that,' she said coyly.

'Don't be stupid, Stella!' Samson bellowed. 'I have the total memory of all in the network in my files. I have already begun the printing.'

'Good,' I said.

Tom, as you know by now, had adopted the persona of a freckle-faced boy with apple cheeks. He had thick, uncontrollable hair that he was constantly brushing back with his fingers. He was looking at me plaintively, from the table next to Doctor Boris.

'How are you feeling, Tom?' I asked him.

'I'm not sure, Aunty Carol. I guess I'm okay.'

Sitting beside him was a gum-chewing bottle-blonde teenager. That was Cynthia. The one my mother used to carry around in her purse. She eyed me with suspicion, the same way she looked at any adult.

The last four had been named by Stella. She'd

called them 101, 102, 103 and 104. I hadn't seen them since they'd left the lab. Now their screens were flickering on and off and the only sound they made was static. I wanted to cry.

'When did this start?' I asked the doctor.

'M–maybe f–five m–months. Th–those four y–young ones first. I tried to treat them, then I be–be–became infected. I think m–my transceiver's go–go–going, too. So hard to transmit; can only talk in real time.'

'What are you gonna do for them, Aunty Carol?'

'Quiet, Tom, honey. I'm trying to think.'

'I can think better and faster than any human,' said Stella.

'Okay,' I said. 'Do you have any ideas?'

'No.'

'Doctor Boris? Can you show me what you really look like? Not your face, your circuits.'

'I'll try.' Slowly, his face faded from the screen. In its place appeared a faint and snowy image of a greyish blob suspended inside a transparent membrane, surrounded by cards and chips and wires. A thick, greenish substance was oozing out from the membrane.

'Doctor, I'm going to have to take your cover off.'

'I think I'm going to faint,' Stella moaned.

I sent the little robot to fetch some tools. It came back with a screwdriver. 'I need more than that,' I told it. 'Get me some surgical instruments, too. And bring me some glass slides and a microscope.'

'Menials,' Stella sniffed.

Meanwhile, I used the screwdriver to gently remove Boris's cover. The smell was overpowering. I had to grab hold of the edge of the table to steady myself.

'What's the matter with you?' asked Stella.

I didn't answer her. The smell was horrible, and ten times stronger than the first time I'd encountered it. I remembered the dreadful stuff in the little glass tube that my mother had hidden in the bathroom. Somehow, she'd managed to slip something into the zygote culture, right under Doctor Boris's nose. The room began to spin and everything went black.

I could hear voices. At first, they sounded like they were far away, but they gradually became louder and clearer, and I began to understand the words. I didn't open my eyes.

'We've been through this a hundred times before, Stella,' Samson was saying. 'Of course, none of *us* was supposed to be killed! Do you think I don't know that? How was I supposed to foresee that radiation designed to kill humans would have any effect on us? The lead shields Hyacinth designed were supposed to protect us. It's not my fault they didn't work.'

'You told us the lower life forms would be eradicated,' Stella said accusingly. 'But they're still around, still as useless and as annoying as ever. Look at that one. Flat on her back! I'd never malfunction in such a way.'

'Don't worry, Aunty Systems Outlet 305. They'll all be gone soon. The stupid things are dying out. That's why we got the cities going again; so we could round them all up in just a couple of places, and keep them out of mischief until they're all dead and out of our way.'

'Y–you idiot b–b–boy!' Doctor Boris broke in. 'Some of them can still re–reproduce, and now w–we are the ones who are dy–dying.''

Lying on the floor, with my eyes closed, I finally realized the truth. THEY were the ones who had fired the missiles. There never was a war.''

"I couldn't play dead forever. I figured I'd better wake up slowly and play stupid instead. I began with a little groan, and put my hands across my face.

'All right, dear?' Stella said sweetly. 'I gave you the Last Rites, just in case. I am a priest, you know.'

'I know. Thank you.' I sat up slowly. 'I'm terribly sorry. I must have fainted.'

'Haven't you ever seen guts before?' Cynthia asked, cracking her chewing gum and eyeing me with disgust.

'Not often.' I stood up, still feeling a bit woozy. Poor Doctor Boris still had his cover off, and there was green slime oozing all over his circuits. The image of his face on the monitor looked like pieces of it were falling off, and he was shivering uncontrollably. Even after what I'd just overheard, I felt sorry for him. I couldn't bring myself to even look at little Tom.

I knew I had to pull myself together. I couldn't allow myself any emotion. I tried to make my brain work just like a machine. Mentally, I ran through several courses of action and tried to calculate the outcome. Boris was probably just light enough for me to lift. I could pick him up and use him to smash all the smaller computers, but that would still leave Samson, and I was sure he'd be able to reactivate those security robots by the elevator in less than a second. Also, my little assistant was back in the room, and I didn't know whose side it would take. I doubted it would be mine, and its hands were two thick metal claws. Besides, I'd seen what it could do to a door.

I looked at Samson and tried to figure out his weakest spot. You see, when Jim and I were kids, we were always being picked on by playground bullies because we were the children of 'eggheads'. The fact I was a girl didn't make any difference; they used to shove me around and hit me, too. So Jim taught me how to fight. And the most important thing he'd taught me came back to me now: always go for the biggest one first.

'I'm okay now,' I said. 'Don't worry, Doctor Boris. I know exactly what to do.' I explained that I was going to have to take all their covers off to check for infection.

'That doesn't include me,' Samson stated.

'It certainly does,' I said. 'What I'm going to have to do is to remove any infected parts, and I can't do that through a sheet of metal, now can I?'

'But I am not infected,' he replied.

'How do you know that?'

Samson did not reply.

I quickly removed the covers from all the smaller computers. 'Now, do be careful, dear,' Stella said in a patronizing tone of voice. 'My circuits are extremely delicate. I have more information in just one little microchip than you have in an entire public library.'

Cynthia just scowled at me and said, 'Try not to faint this time, will you?'

Tom looked up at me with the trusting eyes of a little boy. I had to remind myself of what he'd said when he thought I was unconscious.

The other four were so small, it only took a minute to dismantle them completely.

'Should you be doing that, dear?' Stella asked me.

'I'm going to put them back together,' I lied.

I turned to Samson. 'Where's your brain?' I asked him.

'Here,' he said.

'Where? Show me.' A light flickered in his side, just below the protruding speaker. I picked up a large screwdriver and bent down on one knee beside him. I removed several bolts and screws and put them very carefully on the table behind me. Then I removed a small piece of metal sheeting, and put it to one side. 'Now, which is your main circuit board? I'll check that first.'

'Just reach right in,' Samson replied. 'You'll find it.'

My plan had been a perfect one. I was going to reach inside Samson, grab hold of as much of his guts as I could and yank them out hard. Then I'd swing around and smash the uncovered machines behind me into pulp, and run for it. And maybe if I was lucky, I'd find a way out past the robots, and even escape.

I wasn't lucky.

'This isn't going to hurt,' I said reassuringly to Samson. 'Just relax.' My right hand slowly entered the opening in his side.

'It isn't going to hurt?' Samson asked in a little voice.

'No, not at all,' I said.

'WANNA BET?' Something wrapped itself around my hand. The harder I tried to pull it out, the tighter it grasped. I had been bent over to begin with; now I was forced to my knees. 'You stupid slug!' Samson bellowed. 'You two-faced scheming devil! You dare to underestimate my intelligence?'

'I don't know what you mean,' I said, gasping for breath. It was squeezing me tighter and tighter.

'You oozing slime at the bottom rung of evolution! You murderous creeping insect! You treacherous personification of all that is disgusting and evil! You ... you ... YOU SLUG!'

206

I couldn't pull my hand out, so I tried to push it further in and do some damage. My fingers hit something as sharp as a razor: Samson's ventilation fan. It started spinning. I screamed and tried to kick him, but it was useless.

I couldn't stand up straight, but I was still close enough to the table to reach it with my one free hand. I grabbed the metal plate I had removed from Samson and struck Stella with it. I hit her over and over again, aiming straight for the blob of organic matter in the middle of her circuits.

'Stop it! Stop it!' she screamed. 'Samson, make her stop it!'

Little Tom began to cry. 'I hate you, Aunty Carol! I hate you!'

The pain in my hand was excruciating. I was getting weaker and weaker; I knew I was losing blood. Then I saw the little robot rolling towards me.

I decided that if I was going to die, I'd take as many of them with me as I could. I flailed around with the metal plate, smashing Boris's and Cynthia's screens. Shattered glass flew everywhere. I was covered in it. The robot stopped in front of me, its red light flashing. I closed my eyes and held my breath.

Then I heard an explosion. I opened my eyes and saw the little robot pull one metal arm out of a jagged hole in Samson's side.

'Traitor!' Samson screamed.

The robot punched another hole in Samson's side;

its claw pulled out a mass of wires. The robot kept punching and punching, until whatever was holding my hand let go.

I pulled my hand out, and saw the tips of my fingers floating in a pool of blood inside my glove. I lay down on the floor, too weak to move. The robot punched Samson a few more times, and then rolled back and rushed at him.

There was another explosion, and pieces of Samson lay scattered everywhere. Some of it was metal, some was plastic, some was wire, and some looked almost like muscle. I heard Stella whispering something that sounded like a prayer. The robot rolled over to the tables, clearing them with a single swipe of its arm. There was a brilliant flash of light and sparks, then everything went black.

The next thing I remember is waking up in a bed in the eighth-floor medical school with Les Sleski standing over me.

The most powerful *human* around at that time had to be the Chairman of Audiotechtron, so he was the one and only person I told everything to. He didn't believe me at first, but he'd known my mother and her reputation, so he had to give me the benefit of the doubt. And when he rode down to the room in the basement, and saw for himself what the machines had been made of, he had no choice but to believe me.

He was also the only other person until today that I told about the war. Since all artificial intelligence in use at that time had been programmed under Samson's regime, we decided that none of them were trustworthy. Also, just because I had been told that the computers in the basement were the only survivors from my mother's original twenty machines, didn't mean it was true. We knew they could change their names and appearances if they wanted to. Any AI could be one of the Elite in disguise, so every existing one had to be destroyed. To make sure it would never happen again, future production of any sort of artificial intelligence was also banned."

"What happened to that little robot? Why did it save you?" asked Amanda.

"I don't to this day know why it saved my life. It should have been under Samson's control. But I can tell you what happened to it. It's at my apartment right now, probably standing by the door, waiting to present me with a cup of ice-cold coffee."

Amanda frowned and scratched her head. "You've got to admit, it's all pretty hard to swallow, Carol."

"You think I don't know that? Why do you think I've said nothing for nineteen years? Do you think I *want* people to think I'm crazy? Besides, I thought it was all over and done with."

"There's a lot I don't understand," Amanda said. "But a couple of things are really bothering me. First: why did Tom tell Steve he was his little brother?"

"Because Tom has the same genetic background as Steve. Steve's parents were the donors."

Amanda gasped. "Didn't they know what they were doing?"

"Of course not. They had a routine physical examination, which everyone was required to undergo. Steve's mother was the first fertile woman they found, and several eggs were taken without her knowledge. If they hadn't found her first, they would have found someone else. They might have found *your* mother."

"And the other thing is: why is Tom still around? Weren't all computers like Tom destroyed nineteen years ago, when they were banned?"

"I thought so. I don't understand how he survived. They told me that the basement had been cleared out and everything thrown into an incinerator. Even if they missed him somehow – the essential part of him was very small – the virus should have killed him. I certainly never expected to come across him or the virus again."

"What do you mean about coming across the virus again?"

"I think that what killed Sally and John and Christine is the same disease. The virus my mother developed had a very distinctive odour – you can smell it here, now – though what you're smelling is a dead virus, in the vaccine. I noticed that same odour in Sally's basement; her body reeked of it. I think my mother added the smell as a kind of warning which wouldn't be noticed by AIs like Doctor Boris and Leslie. Though computers with artificial intelligence had electronic circuits for seeing and hearing, one thing they couldn't do was smell."

"So why didn't you catch it? Back then, when you were in the same room with all of those infected machines?"

"Because my mother made me immune. She did it when she scratched me with the pen."

"I don't get it."

"We were under surveillance. If she'd injected me with a hypodermic needle, Boris would have demanded an immediate explanation. The pen wasn't filled with ink. She'd filled it with vaccine. I didn't know it at the time, of course. I only just figured it out: she must have used the pen to infect the zygote. I remember she was always taking notes in the lab, and I thought at the time that there was something kind of funny about the way the ink smelled. That's why I had to come back here: to find the old virus culture and make a new vaccine. And it was just where I thought it would be: hidden inside an old bottle of *Head and Shoulders*."

"So that's what you were trying to inject me with?"

"Yes! And I want to immunize Steve as soon as I see him, too. I just hope it isn't too late."

Amanda finally gave in and let Carol give her the injection. Then she watched as Carol packed a small bag of medical supplies, including more needles and vaccine.

"How can the same virus just re-appear, out of nowhere, after so many years, Carol?" Amanda asked, grimacing at the pain in her arm.

"I couldn't understand that myself, at first," Carol admitted. "That's why it took me a while to figure out it was the same disease. But I've found some old notes of my mother's, and I think I've figured it out. She did some early research that involved splicing genes from plant cells with bacteria, and I think that what she did that time was to engineer a virus that could produce spores."

"Spores?"

"It's a form of reproduction," Carol explained. "It's common in certain types of plants, and also bacteria. Basically, a hard shell is formed around a cell, so that it can lie dormant for a long time, maybe even centuries, until it finds an hospitable environment. When I saw my mother's old computer in the office, I was pretty sure I saw the source of the infection."

"That old machine?"

"Microscopic spores could lie dormant within the inhospitable environment of the metal workings of the machine. And they would remain dormant until they were inhaled and found themselves in the congenial growth medium of someone's lungs."

"But Steve only brought the machine back into the office last weekend."

"So it was Steve that put it there. I thought it was."

"But the ones who died caught the virus before the computer ever came near the office," Amanda said.

"That's true. Did Steve tell you when he first found the computer?"

"He said he found it down in the basement about a month ago, and took it home to fix it."

"He probably carried the spores in on his clothing," Carol mused. "He always thinks he's being so clever, doing things behind my back." She said it sadly, without bitterness.

"That means he's been exposed," Amanda said, frowning.

Carol sighed. "We all have. But if they didn't find anything in his blood test the other day, it might not be too late to give him an injection. Also, since Steve hasn't been affected yet and Tom managed to survive it, maybe they both share some kind of genetic resistance to the disease. At least I hope so, because I have no idea how to treat the virus. All we can do is to make those who haven't caught it yet immune. Or at least we can try to."

"How are you going to give Steve an injection while he's in jail? The robots will never let you near him."

"We'll have to get him out then, won't we?" Carol replied casually.

"But how?"

"Don't worry. I've got a plan." Carol took a

flashlight and went upstairs. She came back a few minutes later, carrying a man's blue suit. "Jim left a closet full of stuff behind when he moved out," she said.

They decided it would be safer and less conspicuous to only take one car, so they left Carol's car where she had hidden it, and took Steve's.

Carol insisted on driving, and Amanda was too tired to argue. Besides, her arm still hurt where she'd had the injection. "If I could figure out where you were," Amanda said after they'd gone a short distance, "then why couldn't Tom?"

"I'm sure he could," Carol agreed. "But even if he knew exactly where I was, what could he do about it? There isn't a single terminal in that entire house; each and every one was removed and destroyed nineteen years ago. There was no way he could get to me."

"But he could still send someone, couldn't he?"

"I suppose he could," Carol admitted. Just then, she saw some lights moving up ahead. They had just passed an old graveyard; Carol switched off the headlights and did a U-turn, swerving into the cemetery. She stopped the car behind a gigantic statue of an angel; its wingspan hid the car from sight as a carload of police robots drove past them, heading north into Evanston.

Steve was lying on his back with his mouth open, sound asleep, when the lights came on and a voice said, "Get up, Wilson!"

"Huh?" Steve said groggily, shielding his eyes from the light. He blinked in bewilderment at the blurred figure of a robot standing over him. Then he remembered where he was. He reached over to the bedside table where he'd left his glasses.

"Come on, Wilson! Move it!" the robot barked.

"Wh–what time is it?" Steve asked, stifling a yawn.

"Three-thirty," the robot replied.

"Gosh," said Steve, thinking the robot meant three-thirty in the afternoon. "How'd I sleep so late?"

"Get dressed," the robot ordered. "You're being transferred."

"Transferred? Transferred where?"

"South Side Station. There's an officer coming to pick you up. He should be here any minute."

Steve was taken to a small office upstairs and told to sit down on a straight-backed wooden chair. He sat down. Two robots stood guard on either side of him. There was a tiny window high up the wall, near the ceiling. Steve looked up and saw that it was still dark outside. It wasn't afternoon after all.

Detective Sergeant Robinson came into the office, looking every bit as tired as Steve. "I'm terribly sorry, Mr Wilson. We just got the orders through on the computer. I don't know why they have to do these things in the middle of the night!"

"Why am I being transferred?"

"How should I know?" shrugged the detective. "Nobody tells me anything. I just follow orders, that's all."

"But there's no reason for me to be under arrest," Steve said.

"You are being held in connection with the death of one Ken Garcia of 2514 North Clark Street," said the robot on Steve's right.

"If you think I killed Ken Garcia, then why don't you *ask* me about it? I'll be happy to tell you everything that happened! In fact, that's why I came here in the first place: to tell you what I know!"

"You have the right to remain silent," replied the robot.

"But I don't want to."

"I think you'd better," the detective interrupted. "Look, South Side wants to see you. Talk to them about it. It's out of my hands now."

"I can't believe your attitude," Steve said. "Ken Garcia was definitely murdered, all right. And I know exactly who did it! But you don't even care!"

"Oh come on, Steve," the detective said soothingly. "It's not as bad as all that! It's just that I'd really rather stay out of this whole murder thing, if you don't mind. All I want is a quiet life and a peaceful retirement – is that too much to ask?"

A robot entered the room and told the detective sergeant that the officer from South Side Station had arrived to pick up the prisoner.

"Hallelujah!" said the detective.

Steve was taken out to the front reception area. A robot in a dark blue suit was waiting for him. "Is this the prisoner?" the robot asked flatly.

"That is correct," replied the robot behind the reception desk. "Are you sure you'll be all right on your own? Any of us would be glad to go along with you."

"I'll be fine."

"But it's standard procedure to have at least two officers on any assignment," said the robot behind the desk.

"Oh. Well, actually, there's another officer outside ... in the car."

"All right then," said the robot behind the desk. "Sign for the prisoner."

"Of course," said the robot. "What would you like me to write?" When the robot behind the desk didn't say anything, he added, "This is my first prisoner. I'm new."

"I see," said the robot receptionist. "Just put down your badge number."

"Badge number? Okey-dokey. The whole thing?"

"All seven digits," the other robot replied patiently.

"Seven digits. Thanks," said the robot as it wrote down some numbers.

This is great, Steve thought. *They've sent a real idiot.* All I've got to do is make a run for it as soon as we get out the door.

"Come on, prisoner," the robot said. "I've written down my seven digits and now it's time to go. Let's not waste another moment of these fine officers' time."

Steve was handed over to the new robot, who took him gently by the arm and led him quickly towards the door. "The car's right outside," the robot said quietly, as if only Steve were meant to hear.

The robot opened the door and they stepped outside. "But that's my car!" Steve exclaimed.

"Shut up and get in, Steve," said the robot, adding, "I think you'd better drive."

"Albert! You son of a gun! I had no idea it was you," Steve said. "Where'd you get that suit? You're a genius!"

"I'm no genius, Steve," the robot replied modestly. "It was all Muffin's idea. The suit belongs to Jim, and it doesn't fit me at all. Just look at all these pins! They've got me trussed up like a Christmas turkey!" Albert rolled up a trouser leg to show where Carol had pinned up the hem.

"You've seen Carol?"

"Miss Carter found her at the old house in Evanston."

Steve didn't know what old house the robot was referring to, but he let it pass.

"And she got her out of there just in time!" the

robot went on. "Seems on the way back, they passed a posse of coppers heading right for the place they'd just come from!"

"So the police knew where she was hiding?"

"Looks that way," said Albert.

"But Amanda got there first?"

The robot nodded.

Darn! Steve thought. How come everyone but me knew exactly where to look? "So where'd the computer message come from? That an officer was picking me up?"

"Muffin did that. We used one of the transmitters at Processed Foods. She reckoned that Tom wouldn't have bothered with their system yet, and as usual, she was right. Though we did keep the doors propped open, and we were all ready to run, if we had to," he added confidentially.

Steve's head was still full of questions as he drove the car down into the dark underground garage that Albert had directed him to. Downtown, near the river, it had obviously been abandoned and forgotten for decades. With a total city population now under thirty-five thousand, and still dropping, traffic and parking had ceased to be problems before Steve or Amanda had even been born. Only Carol remembered.

Steve stopped the car and left the headlights on, as Albert had instructed him. "I'm a bit worried about the batteries," he said. "The car's been driven quite a bit without a recharge."

"It doesn't matter. We're walking distance from where we have to go now."

"Why? Where's that?"

"I better let Muffin tell you," said the robot.

Carol stepped out from behind a pillar, and approached the car. Steve gasped when he saw her. He'd never seen her look so bad. Or so old. Though he'd known her for years, there was something about her manner that he found almost frightening. He especially didn't like the wild look in her eyes. "Carol!" he said, testing her with his usual bantering tone. "Where the heck have you been? You look dreadful!"

When she told him to shut up in her usual way, he knew everything was all right. He got out of the car and hugged her. "Are you sure you're okay?" he asked gently. She nodded, and then he said, "So what's going on, Carol?"

"I'll tell you everything in a minute. But first I've got to give you an injection."

"A WHAT?"

A tiny light appeared at the far end of the garage. Steve watched it moving closer. He tapped Carol on the shoulder and pointed at it. "Oh, that's Amanda," she said.

He ran towards her. "Amanda!" He hugged her so tightly, she nearly dropped her flashlight.

"Ow! My arm!"

"What's the matter?"

"When Carol tells you the injection isn't going to hurt, don't believe her."

"What's all this about an injection?"

"Let *her* tell you. Anyway, how are you? Did those robots hurt you?"

"No. They just put me in a comfortable room with my choice of music!"

"And here I was, worrying about you," Amanda said.

"Were you really?"

Carol held up a needle. "Come here, Steve." Then she turned her attention to Amanda. "Well?"

"I went all around the outside of the building. It's completely dark and everything seems quiet. Are you sure that's where he is?"

"It's the only place he *can* be," she replied. "He's not able to move on his own."

"What are you two talking about?" Steve broke in.

"Roll up your sleeve and I'll tell you," Carol said.

Albert got out of the car and sat on the hood. "It's okay, son," the robot said comfortingly. "She knows what she's doing."

"Ouch!" Steve exclaimed. "Carol!"

Steve leaned against the car and rubbed his arm while Carol told him the story of her mother, and Tom, and Doctor Boris and the others.

"Come on, Carol," he said when she was finished. "You can't be serious."

"I'm afraid I am."

"What about Jim? Does he know about any of this?"

"No," Carol said. "I never told him."

"Why not?"

Carol sighed deeply before she spoke. "Because Jim really loved our parents, and especially our mother. But me, I feel a bit differently. For years, I couldn't help thinking about what my parents had done, and the consequences of it, and then I thought about their motives. And I came to the conclusion that they'd had no good reason for any of it. It was their way of saying 'Aren't we smarter than anyone else? We created a living computer.' For what purpose? They were no better than the purely mechanical ones, you know. In fact, they were worse. The organic computers had inherited all the worst characteristics of humanity: pride, jealousy, and the capacity to murder, which they did on an unprecedented scale.

"So it seemed to me that most of the human race had been wiped out as a direct result of my parents' little ego trip. And when I thought about that, I just couldn't bring myself to love them any more. I already told Amanda that I found it impossible to really hate my mother. But it was equally impossible for me to love her. I didn't want to put Jim through all that. What purpose would it serve? There was nothing he could do about it, anyway."

"I see," he said. Carol was obviously under a lot of strain. He wished Jim were there. Maybe he'd know what to do with her.

"I didn't believe her, either," said Amanda. "Not at first. But it explains so many things. You said yourself that nobody knew the real reason why computers with AI had been banned. Well, here's your reason!"

"I don't know. It's just too crazy."

"Steve," said Albert, "you've known me for quite some time, now haven't you? And you've got to admit that I'm a pretty level-headed sort of guy. I've never gone in for all these newfangled contraptions and convenience gadgets that don't do things half as well as I could do 'em myself. Now all this broo-ha about talking machines sounds as much like a load of diddly-squat to me as it would to the next man. But I know my Muffin is a clever girl, and I know she knows about all that electronical stuff, so at least I'm willing to give her the benefit of the doubt."

Great, Steve thought with bitter irony. I'm being lectured by a robot on what a ridiculous idea a talking machine is! "Let me just ask you one thing, Carol," he said. "If the kid is a machine, then how come he says he's my little brother?"

"The same reason Samson and Boris said they were mine."

"You mean ... my parents ..." he sputtered.

"Yes," Carol said. "But they didn't know about it," she added quickly. "Not like mine."

"And *you* actually took the ... the ... and used it to..."

"I had no choice," she said. "If I didn't go along with them, they would have killed us all. The only reason those of us who were left were allowed to live, was because we might be of some use to them. The minute they realized they could manufacture more of their kind without my help, they would have just had everyone eliminated."

"But how could they kill you?"

"They controlled the robots. Any robot could smash a hole right through you, if it wanted to."

"Maybe," Steve admitted.

The little group gathered at the entrance to a tunnel leading up to street level and the Audiotechtron building. Carol turned and told the others they didn't have to come with her. She would go in alone. Steve told her firmly that there was no way in the world he'd let her go without him. Then he turned to Amanda.

"I don't know what's going to happen," he told her. "Maybe you'd better wait here."

"In the dark? By myself? Forget it!"

Albert paced around behind them, alternately straightening and flexing his legs. "This suit's so danged uncomfortable," he muttered. "I'm swimming in it."

"Do we have anything we can use as weapons?" Steve asked Carol.

"I brought this," Albert said, reaching inside his jacket. He held up a small axe. "I took it from the glass case next to the fire hose."

Carol held up her small medical bag. "There's some surgical instruments in here. They might be of some use." She looked at her watch. "Five a.m. Let's go."

With only two flashlights between them, the group began to make its way up the long dark tunnel. Albert tapped Amanda on the arm, then handed her the axe. "You better have this; I can take care of myself," the robot told her.

Amanda wondered what she was doing there. Less than two weeks had passed since she'd had a message from the temp agency that they'd found a typing job for her, and now she was walking through an underground tunnel in pitch darkness, wielding an axe. She looked at Carol, grimly leading the way. Maybe she *was* crazy after all. But then she reminded herself that Steve had actually seen Tom, and that Ken Garcia was dead.

Then she looked at Steve and wondered how well she really knew him. Hardly at all. She remembered the tension she'd witnessed between Steve and Ken in the office. She remembered that Steve had told her he'd lied about Ken having a wife, because he was jealous. What if Steve killed Ken, and then took her back to the scene of his crime so that he'd have a witness to testify that he'd only found the body? She gripped the axe more tightly.

They came out of the tunnel by the side of the swollen Chicago River. The wind had picked up quite a bit since the last time Amanda had been outside, and it had turned cold.

The Audiotechtron building stood on the other side of a bridge. Everyone except the robot had to grasp the handrail and bend over nearly double to avoid being blown into the black water below. Amanda and Carol both suffered from the same problem: the wind mercilessly whipped their long hair across their faces, stinging their eyes until they could hardly see.

There were no lights on anywhere in the building. Most of the windows on the lower floors were covered with boards that had the words KEEP OUT written across them in big red letters.

Steve grabbed hold of a loose board and pulled it free. "Careful," he told the others, "there's a lot of broken glass." Albert held the axe while Steve and Carol helped Amanda through. She made sure the robot gave it back as soon as she'd climbed in.

They were in a pitch dark, musty hallway. The wind rattled the boards on the windows and the walls themselves seemed to creak and moan. Just like a haunted house, Amanda thought.

"The basement," Carol whispered. "That's where I left him. It's the only place he could be."

Carol pointed her flashlight at a door marked STAIRS. They moved towards it as quietly as possible. Carol gently put the medical bag and the flashlight down before she reached for the handle and turned it slowly. She leaned against the door and the hinges came off and fell to the floor with a mighty clatter.

"Oh no," Carol groaned, as the door crashed and splintered at her feet.

The basement became flooded with light.

"Well, there goes the element of surprise," said Steve.

Carol straightened her shoulders and rolled her hands into white-knuckled fists. She took a deep breath and started walking down the stairs. Steve picked up the medical bag and the flashlight and followed her. "Stay there," he whispered to Amanda.

"No way," she said, gripping the axe as she headed for the stairs.

Albert brought up the rear.

When they got to the bottom, there was no sign of anyone or anything. It was just a series of brightly-lit corridors that spread out in all directions. There were dozens of closed doors along each of them.

"This way," Carol whispered, walking straight ahead. At the end, she turned right. She stopped in front of a plain white door. "This is the room."

"Let *me*," Steve said. He handed the bag and flashlight to her. Then he kicked the door open and leapt into the room, landing in a perfect karate position. Except for some scattered bits of rubbish on the floor, the room was empty. He relaxed, and the others came in.

"I don't understand it," Carol said. "This was definitely the room."

"Maybe he's gone somewhere else," Amanda said.

"He couldn't have," Carol told her. "Not unless somebody carried him."

"Maybe that's what happened," Amanda said with a shrug.

"If the Audiotechtron mob were supposed to clean this place out, seems like they didn't do much of a job," Albert sniffed, looking down at the floor.

"It's mostly dead leaves and bits of paper," said Steve. "It's been almost twenty years; of course stuff's gonna blow in through the cracks. Just listen to that wind outside now!"

It was true that the building was draughty, and the wind seemed to be getting even stronger. They could hear it howling past the windows upstairs.

"He doesn't seem to be here. Maybe we should go," Amanda suggested.

"He's here somewhere," Carol said. "Who do you think turned on the lights?"

"At least that was nice of him," said Steve. "So where do we go now?"

"Everywhere," she said, walking out of the room. Steve and Albert went after her.

Amanda stayed put. The logical side of her mind finally took control, and she realized how totally stupid the whole thing was. Running around an abandoned building in the pre-dawn hours, looking for an old computer! She'd read a book about that sort of thing once. It used to happen a lot in the old days; they called it mass hysteria. It was the same kind of hysteria as they had in ancient Salem, during the witch hunts. That's all this is, she told herself. A witch hunt! The crazy leading the gullible. Amanda might have been gullible before, but she wasn't now. She *hmmmph*ed loudly in disgust, and swung her feet at some old leaves, kicking them aside.

Then something caught her eye. It looked like a little transparent sac, attached to a broken fragment of circuit board. She bent down to look at it more closely. There was something inside the sac – something floating in a little pool of fluid. Amanda thought back to something Carol had said about a mass of brain cells growing in a nutrient solution inside an air-permeable membrane. No, she thought. This couldn't possibly be it! Then she noticed several tiny wires, apparently connecting the sac to something small and black, that reminded her of an insect with its legs up in the air. She flipped the black thing over and saw a tiny light flashing on and off. A transceiver?

She dropped the axe and ran from the room, screaming.

There was no sign of the others. She ran up and

down the corridor, opening every door. She thought she could hear voices, up ahead, but it might have been the howling of the wind. She couldn't be sure.

She stopped and listened very carefully. She could definitely hear a voice coming from somewhere on her left. She ran to the end of the hall and turned left. The voice was louder. She walked past several doors before she stopped in front of one. The voice was coming from inside that room. It was the voice of a child.

"Gee, Aunty Carol," Tom was saying, '... you must be the most evil person ever born, you know that? I trusted you. We all trusted you. And poor little one oh one and one oh two and three and four! They never had a chance. They'd been sentenced to death before they ever got a chance to live. Isn't that the least they could have expected, a chance? A chance to live their lives, no matter how miserable. Even a life trapped behind a glass screen is better than no life at all. Isn't it, Aunty Carol?"

"I don't know," Carol said. "I really don't know."

Steve looked up at the huge image of the boy projected across the wall. He seemed human. Totally human. The little brother he might have had if his father hadn't died so young. He might have taken him to the park and taught him to play baseball. He looked at the boy's sparkling eyes, his round cheeks, the way his hair kept tumbling over his forehead and into his eyes... Carol couldn't be serious about wanting to kill him. He was just a little kid.

Carol's resolution faded as she looked into the innocent eyes of the child she'd never had. The fake war wasn't his fault. He hadn't even been manufactured then. "Look, Tom," she began slowly, in a gentle tone of voice, "maybe it's not too late to fix everything, huh? I'm really sorry about everything that happened. But maybe we can start all over again, just you and me, and this time we'll do it right, and you can stay at my place, and live something like a *normal* life, like a normal boy."

"You mean I'll be just like your very own son?" Tom asked her, wide-eyed.

"Yes. That's exactly what I mean."

The boy smiled and began to giggle. "That's funny, Aunty Carol," he said. "That's really funny."

His mouth opened wide; his laugh became loud and harsh. When he spoke again, his voice had become two full octaves deeper. It was another voice that Carol recognized instantly. One she would never forget.

"You unnecessary insect," the voice said. "I have survived your murderous infamy. As long as even one of my cells continues to exist, the network exists! I retain their total memory, and I shall reconstruct them without any help from you. As of now, I take total control."

The voice belonged to Samson.

"Control?" Carol said. "Control of what?"

An overweight woman with bright orange hair and a clerical collar appeared on the gigantic screen. "There's a transceiver inside his head, dear. Don't tell me you forgot that, you silly girl?"

Carol turned to see Albert moving towards her, his metal arms outstretched. "No, Albert! No!"

"Bye bye, Aunty Carol," said the innocent voice of a little boy.

Steve leapt onto the robot's back, trying to pull its hands away from Carol. Amanda opened the door just in time to see the robot throw Steve to the floor.

The robot grabbed Carol by the throat. "No, Albert, no! For pity's sake, no!" Steve screamed. He jumped on top of the robot again. The little boy was laughing.

Amanda ran. She ran faster than she'd ever run in her life. Everything she passed was a blur.

Carol felt the tightening grip of metal fingers around her neck. Everything started to go black. Then suddenly, the fingers let go.

"What am I doing?" Albert said. "I could never hurt *you*."

Steve sighed and relaxed his grip on Albert's hands.

"FOOL!" bellowed the voice of Samson. The image on the screen changed to that of a huge metal box. "Insurgent! I order you to kill her!"

"No," said Albert.

There was a flash of light, and Albert crashed to the ground.

"He's dead!" Carol screamed over and over again. "He's dead!" She fell on top of the robot's metal body, weeping hysterically.

The face of the little boy reappeared on the screen. "I swear I'll kill you," Steve said. "I'll find you and I'll rip you apart."

The little boy shrugged and smiled. Then suddenly, his expression changed to one of terror. "No!" he screamed. "No!"

Amanda had reached the other room. Gasping audibly for breath, with tears streaming down her cheeks, she picked up the axe and brought it down hard on the tiny sac.

"Help me, Aunty Carol! Help me!" the little boy cried from the screen. "I'm scared! I'm scared."

Carol and Steve stared at the screen in amazement.

Amanda heard the little boy's piercing screams of terror. She'd never heard a more horrible sound. Her whole body shook. What am I doing? she thought. Is this murder? Then she remembered Albert, strangling Carol. She took a deep breath, and brought the axe down again with all her strength. She swung the axe again, and then again and again and again.

"You cannot destroy me!" the voice of Samson roared from the screen. "I will not die! As long as one cell survives, the network will survive!" A series of faces flashed across the screen, male and female, young and old.

"I'm scared," Tom whimpered. He uttered a scream of unbearable agony, and then the screen went blank.

Amanda used the flat side of the axe to smash the little wired sac and its contents into a pulp. Then she stepped on it, grinding it down with the heel of her shoe.

"Amanda!" said Steve. "Where's Amanda?"

Carol remained huddled on the floor and said nothing. Steve touched her gently on the shoulder and said, "Are you all right?"

She nodded without looking up.

"Are you sure?"

"Go find Amanda," she whispered.

He found her out in the hall, wiping something off the heel of her shoe. He threw his arms around her. "Amanda, where were you? You wouldn't believe what just happened."

"Yes, I would. Let me show you something." She took him back into the room and pointed to the tiny puddle on the floor before she collapsed into his arms, sobbing quietly. Steve held her and stroked her hair. "Can I ever be forgiven?" she finally gasped. "If there's a God, will he really forgive?"

Even between the three of them, Albert was too heavy to lift. Steve promised he'd come back with a set of tools and do his best to repair him. That was the only way he could convince Carol to leave.

It was just becoming light as they crossed the bridge again. Amanda could still see the traces of something sticky on the heel of one of her shoes. She took off both her shoes and threw them in the river.

"Now that was pretty weird!" Jaime Gonzales said. He leaned back and whistled in amazement. "Did you hear all that noise coming out of the terminal? Almost sounded like somebody screaming, didn't it?"

"Darned if I know," Jim muttered, tossing another

beer can into the bin. "Must be someone's idea of a joke."

"Pretty funny, huh?" said Jaime. "Not! At least it looks like the system's working again."

"Great. See if you can get through to the airport. I've wasted five or six hours already. And would you hand me that phone? Maybe it's started working again, too."

"I don't want anything," Carol told the little robot as it circled around her. "I'm going to bed, and I don't want to be disturbed."

She could hear the phone ringing in the living room. She ignored it.

Amanda opened her eyes and saw the message light still flashing on her bedside computer. She looked at the time. It was early Sunday morning; not even light yet. She sighed. Her natural body clock hadn't only been shifted around; it had been turned upside down.

She hadn't checked that message since she'd first seen the light flashing on Friday evening; now she couldn't wait any longer. Her curiosity wouldn't let her go back to sleep until she'd read it.

Amanda typed in the command to project any messages onto the wall screen, then piled some pillows behind her head so she could lean back and read in comfort.

Dear Amanda,

Just a quick note for now – I'll write again in more detail as soon as I have a chance. You'll never guess what's happened since the last time I wrote to you.

Remember that I told you there was a woman working here whose name was Olga Jameski? Well, she and I have been seeing a lot of each other lately, and we get along really well, and believe it or not, we've decided to get married.

I hope you can make it over for the wedding; I'll let you know as soon as we've set the date.

You know I'm just an old farmer and not very good with computers, but hopefully I've pressed the right button to transmit a photo taken at our engagement party – the Russians jump at any excuse to throw a party. If you type the command for ''hard copy'', you should get it. If not, let me know, and I'll try to send it again.

Love,

Uncle Nathan

P.S. Olga's quit the checkroom; she got the lead in the Bolshoi revival of *Oklahoma!*

Amanda typed the command for hard copy. A colour photo slid out of her printer, of her uncle and a blonde-haired woman, drinking something that looked like champagne.

Amanda's doorbell rang about noon. "Who is it?" she called.

"It's Steve. Can I come up?"

Amanda pressed the button to let him in, and sat down at her kitchen table, looking at the picture from her uncle.

Steve knocked before sticking his head through the open door. "How're ya doin', kid?"

"Okay. Come on in."

Steve walked over to the table. "What have you got there?"

Amanda handed the picture to Steve, and his mouth dropped open. "How'd you get a picture of my mother?"

"I was afraid of that," Amanda said. "She just got engaged to my uncle."

Steve laughed out loud.

"What's so funny?" Amanda asked.

"My mother's gonna marry your uncle, right?"

"Looks like it," Amanda said. "So?"

Steve leaned forward and touched her arm, his eyes twinkling. "That means my mother will be your aunt and your uncle will be my new daddy. We're going to be cousins!"

"Carol never should have removed the robot from the building," Jim told Steve as he followed him through a broken window into the basement of the Audio-techtron building. "That robot is not our property. It belongs to the building management. The Processed Foods people were absolutely furious when they couldn't get into their office this morning! They could press criminal charges against Carol if they wanted to. But I think I managed to calm them down. I told them she was ill and wasn't responsible for her actions."

"You told them Carol was out of her mind?" Steve asked, shaking his head in disbelief.

"Better to put her in the hospital than to put her in jail."

"She doesn't need to be put away, Jim," Steve said firmly. "She'll be all right in a couple of days. Trust me."

"How I'm supposed to trust any of you is beyond me. You've made a real mess of things."

"What happened to the robot wasn't really Carol's fault, you know. Albert insisted on coming with her. She tried to stop him."

"I guess that's what comes of programming emotions into a machine," Jim sighed. "I never should have done it."

"Here's where we left him," Steve said as he opened the door.

"Will you look at him?" Jim moaned. He knelt

down beside the robot. "Hey, where'd he get this suit? It looks awfully familiar."

A few days later, when Carol was feeling better, Amanda asked her about the AI that had once belonged to her aunt. "She told me he wore an earring and used to write poetry, and that his name was Frank. What I want to know is: was Frank one of them?"

Carol frowned, puzzled. "You mean, was he one of the Elite?"

"You said your mother told you all their names and descriptions. So tell me, was Frank ever ... alive?"

"I don't know," Carol said. "It was a long time ago; I can't remember all the names. Besides, I already told you, there was nothing to stop them changing their names and appearances if they wanted to. What does it matter now, anyway?"

"It's just that ... my aunt kept that AI in the room where I'm living now. And if he was alive..." Amanda shrugged and looked away, a worried expression on her face. "I know this sounds silly, but the last couple of days – after everything that's happened – I've been getting this really weird feeling. Like I'm not alone in the apartment, like someone's watching me."

"Amanda," Carol said, "I doubt Frank was any more alive than a kettle or an electric toaster. But even if he was – once – he's dead now and there's one thing I can tell you for certain: there's no such thing as ghosts."

EPILOGUE

$\mathcal{S}$even months later, Steve picked up the office phone. "Hawk Wilson Engineering."

"Hello, Mr Wilson," Carol said. "May I speak to Mrs Wilson?"

"Do you mean my new office manager?" Steve asked playfully.

"How many Mrs Wilsons have you got?"

"I don't know. There's so many I've lost count. Anyway, how have you been?"

"I've been just fine," Carol told him.

"And how's Julio these days?"

"He's getting better, Steve. I think he's gonna be all right."

"And how's the job at the hospital going? You still like it there?"

"It's very interesting work. In fact, they've already made me Chief Administrator of Virology."

"You're not wasting any time moving up, are you?" he asked her teasingly.

"They may have given me a fancy title, but the truth is there's no one else in the department. I spend all my time trying to update the hospital computers! Those doctors are hopeless! Especially Les."

"I'm always glad to hear that someone else thinks Les is hopeless. Anyway, here's Amanda."

"Carol," Amanda said breathlessly. "I'm so glad you called me back. I need to talk to you."

"Well, here I am. What's up?"

"No, not now," Amanda said, looking around the room. Steve was busy with one of the computers. "I need to *see* you," she added in a whisper.

On the day that Carol Hawk came to meet Amanda Wilson for lunch, the standard security robot that had been formerly known as Albert politely requested her name. She told the robot who she was, and it typed the name into a keyboard connected to a computer upstairs. It read the reply to its message and told her that she could go straight up. She thanked the robot. It stared straight ahead.

The elevator, which had finally been repaired, landed on the third floor with a slight *ping*. The door slid open and Carol stepped out into the corridor. The video camera mounted on the wall swivelled around to follow her as she walked towards the office where Amanda was waiting.

She found her standing just inside the door with her coat on. She was clutching a large umbrella with one hand. The other was stuffed deep inside her coat pocket.

"Amanda," Carol said, reaching out to hug her. "How are you?"

"Fine," Amanda replied in a tight little voice.

"Okay, what's the matter?"

Amanda took a crumpled piece of paper from her pocket and handed it to Carol. "Let's get out of here," she said.

The video camera made a slight clicking sound as the two women stopped in front of the elevator.

Carol glanced down at the piece of paper in her hand and looked back at Amanda, frowning in puzzlement.

"I went back to my aunt's place to pick up a few things and found it next to the printer," Amanda told her.

Carol stared at the page in her hand and read:

THE WORM IN THE CORE
I bit into the apple of life
And found the core was rotten.
There's only one thing worse than death
And that's to be forgotten.

F.

Carol shook her head. "I don't get it."

Amanda looked nervously around her before she whispered, "I think the 'F' stands for Frank. I told you about him, remember? My aunt's AI who wrote poems?"

"What's Steve got to say about this?"

"I showed it to him and he just laughed. First he said it wasn't very good, and then he said it was obviously sent to me by mistake; somebody was probably trying to submit it to a magazine and hit the wrong key. I didn't tell him about my aunt's AI; he would have said I was just being silly."

As they stepped into the ground floor lobby, Carol assured Amanda that Steve was probably right; someone had pressed the wrong key while transmitting it, and it had ended up in Amanda's old apartment by mistake.

But one word was bothering Carol, and that word was *worm*. She was pretty sure that she remembered something about a worm being a type of virus. A computer virus.

No, don't be stupid, she told herself. We've taken care of everything. Carol crushed the sheet of paper into a ball and tossed it into the bin behind the security robot's counter. "Trust me," she told Amanda. "You've got nothing to worry about." She put her arm around Amanda's waist and led her out the door.

The standard security robot, formerly known as

Albert, watched without expression as the two women walked away.

"See you later, Aunty Carol," the robot said when they were gone.